QUICK BEFORE
THEY CATCH US

Mark Timlin

QUICK BEFORE THEY CATCH US

NO EXIT PRESS

First published in Great Britain by No Exit Press, 1999.
18 Coleswood Road, Harpenden, Herts, AL5 1EQ, England.

Copyright © 1999 Mark Timlin

http://www.noexit.co.uk

A CIP catalogue record for this book is available
from the British Library.

ISBN 1-901982-67-X
Quick before They Catch Us hb

1 3 5 7 9 10 8 6 4 2

Composed in Palatino by Koinonia, Manchester
and printed and bound in Great Britain.

To my friend Judith
and to
Peter Walker, for his
invaluable input

One

IN AN EVER changing world, it's good to know that some
things are constant. So, when I'm not hanging around some
low life dive looking for an even lower life individual who's
run out on his child support maintenance or defaulted on a
county court order or something similar, then Friday night is
ruby night. A good medium to hot curry with some saffron
rice and a few pints of lager before a large water ice followed
by a couple of Irish coffees made with real cream, not
something out of a spray can.

You can always judge a restaurant by its Irish coffee, and as
I've mentioned before, by some strange quirk, Indian
restaurants make the best. I've never been able to figure out
why. The coffee's got to be boiling hot, strong and dark, the
cream cool and fresh, with lots of sugar stirred into the coffee,
not left at the bottom of the glass, and it's got to be a double
measure of spirit. Nothing less will do, and that's all she
wrote.

And lately, the place to go for those thick and sticky treats
has been Luigi's. Not that it's called Luigi's any more, but it
was a first rate purveyor of pizza and pasta for so many years
before Luigi took himself and his wife and all the little Luigis
and Luigiettes back to Italy to live the full and prosperous
lives they all deserved, that I can't bring myself to call it
anything else. Even though nowadays it's been renamed
Curry Nights and the white walls have been painted a gentle
peach to match the new tablecloths and napkins and
succulent plants strong and thick enough to hide a family of
monkeys entwine themselves between the tables like you
were in some exotic jungle on the Indian sub-continent. Real
high class, I'm sure you'll agree.

But that's not the reason I still go there regularly and can
call the waiters by name and always get a good table. No. The
reason I go there is because, at half-nine or so when I'm
slumped back in my chair and the Irish whiskey is beginning
to kick in, the owner comes on in a tight white suit with a
high collar and extravagantly flared trousers spattered with

rhinestones, his hair slicked back in a greasy quiff, the karaoke machine spits out the backing track for *American Trilogy*, and the one, the only, bhangra Elvis in south London karate kicks himself back to Las Vegas *circa* 1969 when the King had made a triumphant comeback with a top five record and a TV show that had broken all viewing records. At least that's what the owner had told me, and who was I to argue with an expert? And he was an expert. On Elvis' life and death and everything in between.

I've never told him, in fact I don't think I've ever told anyone, but I remember exactly what I was doing the night Elvis died. The 16th of August 1977, as clear as if it were yesterday. I was with a whore in west London. Not that I can remember precisely where she lived, I was too pissed for that. But roughly it must've been Chiswick or Hammersmith. That's the only thing I don't remember, the rest's as clear as day.

I was in the job then, a detective-constable, keen as mustard, married to Laura, and living in Kennington, but Judith was yet to be conceived. Still a twinkle as they used to say. I'd been on at the Bailey for a long firm trial and we'd had a result. I had a few drinks after with my colleagues to celebrate, then headed further into town on my own, and as the pubs shut at three in those days I'd found a drinker in Goodge Street that stunk of piss where the barman, a heavy individual, entertained the punters with close-up conjuring tricks.

It said members only on the door, but there was no question of membership. I guess being able to find it was the requisite.

The girl was at the bar drinking gin and tonics and putting the lemon slices in the ashtray in front of her. I asked her why. She told me that then she knew how many she'd had, which was fair enough I suppose. When I started talking to her it was seven, when we left at five-thirty it was fifteen. We went straight into a pub over the road and I almost fell down the stairs when I went for a piss, I was so drunk.

We stayed there till eight and she told me she was on the game then invited me home with her. She was a big girl in a red dress, and underneath she was wearing red French knickers over her tights. I found that out when I put my hand up under her skirt and into her crotch.

I'd forgotten about Laura and the supper that was cooking by then and the girl and I left the pub and hailed a cab and it cost me a fortune. I think there was some trouble with the cabbie on the Westway but fuck knows what.

We got to her flat and it had started raining and inside there was another tart and a young boy of dubious sexuality, and the woman was cooking chicken curry and I had some. Then we got stuck into a bottle of Scotch and the evening vanished.

The girl and I finally got into bed around one and I couldn't get it up. Not a flicker. Not a glimmer. The bird was well pissed off, and I wasn't too happy myself. 'Some nights you can't even give it away,' she said bitterly. I'll always remember that.

I fell asleep for a bit and when I woke up *Riders on the Storm* by the Doors was playing on the radio. It was Radio Luxembourg, remember that?

There was something weird about the whole vibe and I had a horrible feeling the girl was going to come in with a kitchen knife and do me serious injury.

Then on the hour there was a news bulletin. Elvis had been found dead, it said, and after that it was nothing but his old records.

I got up and got dressed and left without saying goodbye. It was pissing down outside, thunder and lightning and all sorts and I didn't have a coat. I took shelter under a tree in someone's front garden. Then I saw a cab with its light on and stood in the middle of the road so it had to stop.

The cabbie was pissed off too. Said he lived about a minute away and was on his way home. I told him he should've turned off his light and showed him my warrant card and threatened to report him to the carriage office if he didn't take me. I was in the cab by then and he took me as far as the Houses of Parliament and no further, so I had to walk the last bit.

It was almost four by the time I got home and Laura wasn't best pleased. I told her Elvis was dead, and fell into bed beside her and slept till noon.

She never asked me where I'd been and I never told her.

She's dead too now, but our marriage was over long before. I'm sorry for the way I treated her, but being sorry doesn't cut it. Not in my book. Not any more.

That particular Friday, over twenty years since Elvis had overdosed on prescription medicine and junk food, I was planning to take my new chum Melanie Wiltse out to dine and drink and sing along to *In the Ghetto, Blue Moon of Kentucky* and other Elvis favourites. I'd met Melanie on my case: I'd been hired to find her best friend by her best friend's husband and we'd become close. I liked her and we were becoming something of an item. She still had her flat in Walthamstow, but because she worked in Blackfriars and the Thameslink station was only a short stroll down to the bottom of my road and would deposit her at her desk in less than thirty minutes, she seemed to have become a kind of room mate.

I knew that when I found my shaving gear consigned to the tiny window ledge in my minuscule shower room and her make up victoriously claiming the shelf above the sink.

I read somewhere that we are all just nine meals way from the breakdown of society. Three days from total anarchy and murder in the street. I reckon that when you find half a dozen pairs of clean women's knickers in a M&S bag on the sideboard next to your bed you're only nine meals and three days away from total female domination.

But then – who gives a shit?

Of course recently, she's been getting on my case to make things more permanent. But then that's what women do when they get into a relationship with a man. God made them that way.

So there I was that afternoon, safe and warm in my little flat watching TV without a care in the world, looking forward to an evening of hedonistic pleasure with my new girlfriend, just kicking back without a care in the world except whether to watch Jerry Springer or *The Rockford Files*, not knowing what fate had in store for me before I got as far as ordering the chicken korma and the Kingfisher lager.

Two

MELANIE CAME IN around six-thirty that particular evening, all fresh paint job, flowery perfume and cold autumn air from the street outside, clutching four Tesco Metro shopping bags and a black leather shoulder bag, shucked off her coat and came over and gave me a kiss. I think I forgot to say she had a spare key. Female domination. Remember?

She smelt good, she felt good, so like I said, who the fuck cared if she'd moved in on me?

'Hello duck,' she said. 'Had a good day?' I knew she was in a good mood when she called me duck.

'*Are You Being Served?* from the 1970s, *The New Avengers* from the 1980s and *Between the Lines* from the 1990s,' I replied. Jesus, but I love satellite television.

'You watch too much TV. You should get out into the world and earn some money.'

'I've got some money. When that's gone I'll earn some more. And I'm not that fond of the world. It's all *too* real out there.'

'You could do with a dose of reality.'

'I've had plenty, remember? The last dose of reality I had left me in hospital for a couple of weeks. I'm just happy to sit here and chill out with a bottle of beer and the TV.'

'Ever heard the story of the ant and the grasshopper? GRASSHOPPER.' She pulled her eyes slitty and pronounced it like the priest from *Kung Fu*.

'And you say *I* watch too much TV,' I said and gave her another hug. 'How was your day?'

'Not bad. Made my bosses a few thousand quid, had lunch with some mates from the office, talked about who's going to bed with who they shouldn't be. Filed my nails, bought some Tampax. Girly things, you know.'

'Tampax. Does that mean PMT's about to strike?'

'Maybe.'

'Hey, Mel. What's the difference between a terrorist and a woman with PMT?' I said.

'Oh good Nick. More public bar jokes.'

'No. Come on, what's the difference?' I pressed. I love to get her at it. I know it's juvenile, but there you go.

'I don't know,' she said patiently and with a thin smile.

'You can negotiate with a terrorist.'

'Cutting edge humour, Nick. You should watch it. You might hurt yourself, you're so sharp.'

'Just a boyfriend joke, Mel. I've got a thousand of them.'

'I just bet you have,' and she pulled off one of her high heeled shoes and threw it. I caught it one-handed.

'You going to stay the weekend?' I asked as she kicked off the other. See, I was glad she was there really. I just thought that sometimes I should put up a token resistance.

'If that's OK with you, and you promise not to tell any more boyfriend jokes.'

'Scout's honour,' I said, giving her a salute with three fingers against my forehead.

'OK, then, I'll stay.'

'Perfect.'

'I brought food.'

'We'll eat that another day. I fancy an Indian tonight.'

'Big surprise. Don't you ever get tired of that bloke and his Elvis impersonations?'

'No. You don't mind, do you?'

'Course not. I wouldn't be here if I did.'

'I'd better take a shower and change before we go then,' I said and got up from the sofa.

'Good idea, you're beginning to smell a bit ripe.'

'Charming,' I said and pulled off the sweatshirt and jeans that I must admit were a few days past their wash-by date and tossed them somewhere close to the laundry basket. I hadn't seen Melanie for a couple of days and had been a bit lax in my personal hygiene. When you've got nothing to do, why bother? On the way through the kitchen dressed just in my shorts I grabbed Mel from behind and gave her a proper cuddle and rubbed my face into her neck.

'Did I say ripe?' she asked. 'I meant rotten. And have a shave, will you? Your beard's like iron filings.'

'But am I still your sex god?' I asked.

'I'll tell you later.'

I went into the bathroom, showered, shaved, rubbed my hair dry, then with a towel round my waist I went to find clean clothes.

'That's better,' she said when I emerged. 'Sex god is a possibility.'

'Thank you *so* much.'

I dressed in fresh underwear and socks, a laundered shirt, pressed chinos and boots and had to admit to myself that it did feel good to be clean again.

'Are we going to drive?' asked Mel whilst I was combing gel into my hair.

'I fancy a walk,' I replied. 'I haven't been out all day, except to get the paper this morning.'

'What a bloody life you do lead,' she said, and found a pair of low-heeled pumps under the sofa and shoved her nyloned feet into them. 'Are you fit then?' she asked.

'Not as fit as you are, darling,' I replied with a leer.

'Don't you ever come up with any new lines?'

'Not when the old ones work so well.'

I pulled on my old Schott leather, put cigarettes, lighter and wallet into the pockets, strapped on my watch and I was ready. Melanie put her coat back on and we left the flat.

Three

I T WAS ONLY about a ten minute walk up to Streatham High Road and we got to the restaurant about half-seven, quarter to eight. It was mostly empty that early and a familiar waiter came trotting over and wished us a very good evening before leading us to our usual table in the corner with a good view of the stage.

We ordered a couple of beers whilst we looked over the menu, but it wasn't the waiter who brought them. Instead it was the boss, the surrogate Hillbilly Cat, Suri Agashe, dressed in the black dinner jacket and bow tie which was his uniform when he wasn't strutting his Elvis stuff, who arrived a few moments later with the bottles and glasses on a tray.

'Good evening Mr Sharman, good evening madam,' he said in his peculiar accent that was somewhere between Bombay and Bradford, as he poured the drinks. Maybe I forgot to mention it. Suri's family had settled up north somewhere when they came to this country, which, to me at least, made his obsession with a fat junkie from Memphis, Tennessee even more peculiar. But to each his own. 'I am so glad you are in this evening,' he continued. 'Mr Sharman, can I see you a moment in private.'

'What for?' I asked. 'Panic in the kitchen. Sorry Suri, my expertise with Indian food stops at Marks and Sparks meals for one in the microwave.'

'No, Mr Sharman. I need a word. I won't keep you for longer than a minute.'

I looked at Mel. She shrugged. 'OK Suri,' I said. 'Where?'

'In the back,' he said, and I pulled a puzzled face at Melanie, excused myself, got up and followed him through the doors that lead to the kitchen area. Inside it smelt warm and spicy. Suri dragged me out into the tiny service area at the back of the restaurant which housed the rubbish bins for the place and believe me didn't smell half as good.

'What's the story, Suri?' I asked when the door to the kitchen was closed and we were alone.

'There is someone coming to the restaurant tonight who

wants to see you,' he said.

'Do I owe him money?' I asked only half jokingly. I've got a history.

'No, no, no. Quite the contrary. In fact it is me who owes him. He is my benefactor. His name is Mr Rajesh Khan.' He said the name almost reverentially. 'It is he who gave me the wherewithal to open this establishment. I worked for him for many years since leaving school. He is down here from Manchester at the moment, and when I told him about you he was most eager to make your acquaintance.'

'What *did* you tell him about me?'

'What you do for a living. A private detective.'

'Semi-retired Suri. Semi-retired.'

'Oh Mr Sharman.' Suri wrung his hands and for one horrible moment I thought he was going to get down on his knees. 'Please see Mr Khan, I beg you. I have told him so much of your exploits and he says you are just the man for the job.'

'Job? What job?' I echoed. 'I'm not sure I'm in the market for a job.'

'Mr Sharman. Just listen to what Mr Khan has to say, that's all I ask. He said he will look in at ten-thirty after my set to see if by chance you dined here tonight. I told him you usually did on Fridays.'

'Just as well I didn't go for sweet and sour pork and Singapore noodles down the road then, isn't it? What kind of job is it anyway?'

Suri raised his right hand to stop further questions. 'It is not for me to say. That is between you and Mr Khan. It is a matter of great delicacy and embarrassment to him, that I do know, and my heart bleeds for my old friend. Just be patient. And naturally this evening's meal for you and your charming lady friend will be on the house.'

'Even if I decline the job.'

'Of course, Mr Sharman. No one could ever accuse me of being an Indian giver.'

I ignored Suri's joke. 'OK,' I said. 'You just keep bringing the Irish coffees and I'll listen to what the man has to say. But Suri – no promises.'

'I understand, Mr Sharman. No promises.'

With that he allowed me to return to Melanie at our table. She had polished off all her beer and half of mine, at the sight of which Suri bustled off to fetch fresh supplies before leaving us to order our meal.

'What was all that about?' asked Melanie when he'd vanished off to get changed for his Elvis spot. 'Did you bounce a cheque here last time or something?'

I told her what Suri had told me. 'Good,' she said when I'd finished and we'd ordered our food from our original waiter. 'I said it was time you earned some money.'

'I haven't taken the job yet,' I said.

'If Suri bribes you with enough liqueur coffee you will.'

A great judge of character was our Melanie. But she wasn't far wrong, and besides I'd been getting lazy and it was about time I did some work for a change. The world was beckoning. But if I'd known what delights it was going to reveal I might just have gone back to my TV.

Four

THE FOOD CAME and it was good. Every speciality of the house including ones we hadn't ordered were piled up in front of us until the table almost groaned with the weight of it. With it came as much beer as we could manage, and afterwards enough Irish coffee to float a battleship. Something told me Suri was trying to soften me up. Suri, or his mentor, or both. Whoever it was, it was working. Especially with Melanie. She was scarfing up the food and drink like it was going to be illegal come midnight.

'This is great,' she said.

'Sure is,' I agreed. 'But remember—'

'I know,' she interrupted. 'A moment on the lips, a lifetime on the hips. Have you got any complaints?'

Looking at her svelte figure I shook my head.

'Then be quiet,' she said and went back to her food.

At nine-thirty as usual, as our empty plates and dishes were whisked away, the already dim lights in the restaurant were turned down even further, the fanfare from *An American Trilogy* thundered out from the PA system, a single spot illuminated the stage and Suri leapt into the light, rhinestones glittering on his one-piece white suit with the high collar and cape, and his hair piled up in a gleaming pompadour. He fell into a martial arts pose and let rip into the microphone he was holding in his right hand. I've got to tell you it cracked me up every time, but I never let it show. Suri took his Elvis Aaron Presley seriously, and when he was around, so did I.

He went through his usual repertoire from *Heartbreak Hotel* to *Polk Salad Annie* with plenty of stops along the way, until he encored with *Unchained Melody*, took a bow to applause from what was by then an almost packed restaurant and left the stage.

'Pretty good,' said Melanie when the lights came up and the usual Ravi Shankar greatest hits came over the speakers, and I noticed that there was just one empty table by the door with a RESERVED sign standing on the tablecloth like a little soldier on guard.

But the table wasn't empty for long. A few minutes after
Suri left the stage, round about half-ten like he'd said, the
front door opened and a large Asian man in an expensive
shiny suit came in flanked by two even larger Asians and
were shown to it by a waiter, and I guessed that Mr Rajesh
Khan from Manchester had entered the building.

A moment later Suri came back, dressed again in his tuxedo,
spotted the newcomers and almost jogged over to them. There
was a whispered conversation and he pointed in my direction
then headed our way. 'That is Mr Khan,' he said in a whisper
when he got to where Mel and I were sitting.

'I guessed,' I said. 'It was a bit like the entry of the
gladiators there for a minute.'

'He asks will you join him?'

'Both of us?'

'No. You alone. The young lady will be fine here.'

'My name's Melanie,' she said. I'd noticed that she didn't
like to be talked about as if she wasn't there. Especially at that
time of the month.

'Miss Melanie,' said Suri. 'My apologies. Another coffee?'

'Don't mind if I do,' said Mel.

'I'll have one too,' I said. 'Will you bring it to his table?'

Suri nodded, I winked at Mel and told her I wouldn't be
long and Suri led me over to where Khan and his party were
sitting.

'Mr Khan sir,' said Suri. 'This is Mr Sharman who I have
told you so much about.'

Khan pushed back his chair and rose to his full height
which was about the same as mine, but he outweighed me by
maybe five stone. I guessed he was fiftysomething, but his
brown skin was smooth and unlined and his thick hair was so
deep a black as to be almost blue. 'Thank you, Suri,' he said,
and Suri bowed and backed away towards the bar.

'Pleased to meet you, Mr Khan,' I said and stuck out my
mitten.

'I'm pleased to meet *you*, Mr Sharman. Forgive me for
interrupting your evening,' said Khan and took my hand in a
strong grip. His accent was middle class and refined. No trace
of Bombay *or* Bradford. He could've been a doctor or a lawyer
or anything along those lines, but with the two minders in
tow I doubted if he was. 'Join me.' He flicked his free hand at

his two companions who got up and did a fast shuffle in Suri's wake. I took one of the vacant seats and Khan sat opposite. 'Did you enjoy your meal?' he asked.

'Very much. I always do.'

'Excellent. It's important to know that my investments are being used wisely.'

'Suri runs a fine restaurant.'

'He had a good teacher. Me. And you enjoy his act?'

'Always. I try not to miss it.'

'Good. He told me you are a Friday night regular. Did he tell you why I wanted to speak to you?'

A little preliminary work and then straight down to business. It struck me Mr Khan was quite a powerful man whatever his business. Or probably because of it. 'No,' I replied. 'Just that you wanted to see me on a private and delicate matter.'

'Then let me explain.' He took a brown envelope from the inside pocket of his expensive jacket and laid it, unopened, neatly in front of him between the unused cutlery. 'I have a family, Mr Sharman. Not a large family. Three children in all, two boys and a girl. They are grown, but they are still children to me. Do you understand that?'

'I have a daughter of my own, Mr Khan,' I replied. 'She's sixteen now. Almost an adult, but I still think of her as a baby.'

'Then you *do* understand. That is very good, it makes what I have to say easier. My children are older. The boys are in their twenties and Meena is eighteen. Just eighteen.'

I said nothing.

Khan undid the envelope and took out some photographs. He separated one from the pile and slid it in front of me. It was a girl. A very beautiful Asian girl. She looked straight into the camera's lens and smiled. It was the kind of smile that would break hearts and it almost broke mine. It made me think of my daughter Judith, and lately that always makes my heart ache. 'That is Meena,' he explained.

'She's lovely,' I said.

'She is. That was taken last year on her seventeenth birthday. She was even more beautiful the last time I saw her.'

I made a puzzled face.

'She is gone, Mr Sharman,' he explained.

'Gone?' I queried,

'Yes, gone.' His hand played with the knife in front of him. There was a heavy gold ring on his little finger.

'Gone where?' I asked. I felt he expected me to.

'I don't know. That's why we're sitting here.'

'Run away?' I said. I remembered when Judith had run away years before and how helpless I'd felt.

'Eloped.' His mouth twisted as he spoke.

'I see,' I said.

'I doubt it.'

'With whom?' I asked.

'With him.' He separated another photograph and passed it to me. It was a bad photo. A Polaroid lit by a flash that made the subject's eyes red like a werewolf's. He was in his twenties, white, with a spiky, Rod Stewart seventies haircut, wearing a T-shirt that showed his upper arms and the tattoo on the left one. In one hand was a pint glass half full of beer, in the other a cigarette.

'Who is he?' I asked.

'Scum. A jailbird who inveigled himself into the life of my family and took the jewel I called my daughter.'

'Called?' I queried. 'Do you think something has happened to her?'

He shook his head. 'You misunderstand me,' he said. 'I mean that she is no daughter of mine until she returns without this… this… man.'

'And does he have a name? This man?' I asked.

'Jeffries.' Khan almost spat the word. 'Paul Jeffries.'

Five

'TELL ME MORE about Paul Jeffries,' I said when Khan seemed to have regained his composure. I was interested, I've got to admit. It was quite a while since I'd had a job, and it was intriguing. Other people's problems always are. And they take your mind off your own. And you don't seem to hear about couples eloping like you used to. Gretna Green is not the place it was.

'He met one of my sons at a club in Manchester some time ago. Sanjay – my younger son. They got friendly.'

'How old is Paul?' I interrupted.

'Twenty-seven.'

'And Sanjay?'

'Twenty-two.'

'And you say that Paul has been to prison.'

He nodded.

'What was he inside for?'

'What wasn't he? Burglary. Car theft. Actual bodily harm and drugs.'

'Quite a record. How do you know all this?'

'I got it out of Sanjay later. Paul had confided in him, but no one thought to confide in me.'

That's families for you, I thought. 'Has Sanjay ever been in trouble with the law?' I asked.

'Of course not.'

'There's no "of course" about it. How about your other son?'

'No. And before you ask, nor has Meena. Now may I continue?'

'Certainly,' I said. 'I just need to fill in the background. Do go on.'

'They started meeting at other clubs on a regular basis. They shared a taste in music. Black American music. Where Sanjay got that from I'll never know.'

I could almost hear the arguments in the Khan household.

'Then Sanjay invited Paul to the house where he met my other son – and Meena of course.'

'Of course,' I said.

Khan ignored me.

'Paul was out of work at the time. As usual, as far as I can understand. He's nothing. An itinerant picking up jobs where and when he can. How he could afford to go around with Sanjay I don't know. From his previous record, by thieving I imagine. Deepak, my elder boy offered him a job in one of the restaurants he manages. A barman. The boys felt sorry for him. Little did they know that behind all our backs he was busily seducing Meena.'

'Was it that cold blooded?'

He looked at me quizzically. 'Meaning?' he asked.

'Do you think he just hung around to…seduce, as you put it, your daughter? Or did they fall in love?'

'Love. Love is nothing. Love is a commodity to be bought and sold like any other.'

I was beginning to take a bit of a dislike to Mr Khan, and if it hadn't been for Suri behind the bar watching our conversation from a distance I think I would've left then.

'I may be an old cynic, Mr Khan,' I said. 'But cynical as I am, I'm afraid I can't agree with you on that one.'

'Sentimental rubbish. Meena was promised to another.'

'Who?'

'The son of a friend from the sub-continent.'

'Did she tell him she loved another?' Even as I said it, the question sounded like something from a Victorian novel. But then Khan's attitude was pretty Victorian. But Meena wasn't my daughter. And I imagined that if Judith had run off with a jailbird I'd be a little Victorian myself. More than a little, in fact.

Khan laughed. The first time he'd done that. *'Tell him,'* he said. 'How could she tell him? She's never even spoken to him.'

It clicked then. 'An arranged marriage,' I said.

'Of course. Like mine and my father's before me, stretching back generations. It is the best and only way.'

'Obviously Meena didn't see that.'

'What does she know?' He raised his voice and slapped the table and people looked, including Melanie. 'She is just a stupid girl whose head has been turned by a little jailbird who talks big and does nothing.'

'He got your daughter,' I observed.

Khan's dark skin turned darker and I thought he was going to lean over and give me a smack like he had the table. But instead he mopped at his face with a napkin. 'I'm sorry,' he apologised. 'I get carried away.'

In an ambulance if you're not careful, I thought. If you go on like that. Off to the cardiovascular unit. 'How long ago did this all happen?' I asked when he'd calmed down.

'Paul Jeffries and Sanjay met maybe eighteen months ago, and he and Meena ran away in July.'

Three months previously.

'Have you heard from them at all?' I asked.

He shook his head.

'Has anyone heard from them? Her brothers for instance.'

'Her brothers are even angrier than I. It was them that Paul Jeffries used the most. Believe me, they would not contact them.'

'She must have friends. Girl friends. How about them?'

'Nothing that I've heard about.'

But that didn't mean it hadn't happened. I knew how teen-age girls like to talk. 'But you've been looking, I presume.'

'Naturally. Her brothers and myself. And friends of the family and business acquaintances. I have a network of people constantly looking. My network reaches far and near.'

'But not far and near enough,' I said.

He didn't reply.

'Have you been to the police?' I enquired.

He shook his head. 'No police. It is bad enough what has happened without involving the authorities. I take care of my own business. And my own family.'

But not this time, I thought. This time you need outside help. 'So what do you want *me* to do?' I asked after a moment. Of course I knew, but I wanted him to tell me. I wanted him to ask, just like a normal father would do.

'I want you to find them.'

'Where do I start?'

'In London. He comes from London. South London, to be precise. Your area of expertise, I believe, Mr Sharman.'

'Does he know you're after them?'

Khan nodded. 'Of course. He knows I won't rest until Meena is home with me where she belongs.'

'Then it's probably the last place he'll come.'

'He'll come here. He's like a rat. He'll return to his nest.'

Suri arrived at that moment with a fresh Irish coffee for me and what looked like a glass of sparkling mineral water with ice and a slice for Khan. But then it might've been a gin or vodka and tonic. What did I know? What did I care?

When he'd gone I leant forward. 'Mr Khan,' I said. 'Tell me something about yourself.'

He looked puzzled. 'Like what?'

'Like what you do.'

'Why?'

'I'm interested. You obviously know a lot about me; tell me a little about yourself.'

'Is this important? I want you to do a job for me. I have the wherewithal to pay—'

I cut him off. 'I'm not interested in your money, Mr Khan. Well, not exclusively. And I do like to know who I'm working for. That is if I decide to take the job,' I added. 'As a matter of fact I'm at a loose end at the moment, and you seem to be important to Suri who I'm very fond of. But the same doesn't go for you Mr Khan. Not in the least. So if you do want me to take the job – indulge me.'

Six

FOR A MOMENT I thought he was going to tell me to piss off, but instead he said. 'You have a very strange way of doing business, Mr Sharman, if I may so so.'

'So I've been told, and believe me it's cost me in the past. Cost me dear.'

'I can believe that. If you really don't care about money then you are a very dangerous man.'

I shrugged.

'Suri told me you were strange. But not exactly how strange,' he said and sipped at his drink. 'But reliable and good at what you do, and I trust his opinion. Very well. A potted history. My family came from Uganda where they'd settled years before. They were merchants. Rich. They sent me here to school. A good school. A very good school. I did well and went to university. I lived the life of Riley. Then Amin sent them packing. With nothing. My university days were over. My father was forced to open a little tobacconist's on Whally Range in Manchester. Not the most salubrious of neighbourhoods. We lived over the shop. My father, my mother, my sister and my four brothers. We worked hard. Sometimes twenty-three hours a day. Soon we had more tobacconists. My brothers and I moved into clothing. Wholesale and retail, and then restaurants. You English love your chicken korma.'

I didn't know if he was having a go.

'That is where I met Suri. He came to me as a sixteen-year-old waiter. I trained him up. There was something about the boy…In time he managed a restaurant for me, then two. Then he wanted to spread his wings. Open his own place. I didn't want him in competition so I told him I'd back him anywhere but Manchester. He decided on London. He is doing well. Another place is in the pipeline. He is not yet thirty. By the time he is my age he will be a big operator. I'm glad he moved south. But I miss him and his silly Elvis music. He is like one of my own sons. But business is business.' He took another sip from his glass. 'Now I am rich. Extremely rich, with a beautiful house in Didsbury, just outside Manchester. That doesn't protect me from traitors from inside. Traitors like Paul Jeffries. But I am rich enough to hire men who can. Men like you. Will that suffice, Mr Sharman?'

I felt like he was rubbing my nose in it, but I just nodded. 'Fine,' I said. 'But one thing still worries me. It's obvious from the way you speak, the way you are, that you are an operator yourself. A big wheel in the Asian community.' He didn't correct me so I went on. 'And it strikes me that London is full of Asians, Mr Khan—'

'A Paki shop on every corner, you mean,' he interrupted angrily.

'That's not quite how I'd put it, but yes.'

'To you English, all Asians are Pakis. Is that not right? Pakis to be used and abused. I wonder why your countrymen treat us thus, Mr Sharman. Don't you remember how it used to be before we came?'

I did as a matter of fact. All shops opening at nine and closing at six with half-days on Wednesday and never being able to get a packet of fags after the pubs closed. 'I remember,' I said.

'You English hate to work. You want to lie in bed all day in your own stink and you hate us for being industrious. I never took a penny from this country and have paid a fortune in taxes, but still I'm a stinking wog. A dirty Paki. So called by people who have never washed and live in places that have never seen a mop and bucket.'

'You don't think much of my countrymen, do you, Mr Khan?' I said.

'No.'

'Then why ask me to work for you?'

'Because you can go where my men cannot.'

'It still worries me. If Paul Jeffries and your daughter know that your network reaches near and far as you put it, then I really think that they'll look for somewhere where Asians are in a minority.'

'They need money. Friends and money. He has family here.'

'Family?'

'His mother.'

'I see,' I said.

'And his brother. Another piece of scum, who works on building sites when he works at all.'

'You're very judgmental if I may say so, Mr Khan,' I said.

'You may say what you like, Mr Sharman. That is your privilege. And I may ignore it or not. That is mine.'

'Fair enough.'

'So are you interested in working for me?'

'I don't know.'

'I'll pay you well. Double your normal fee, whatever that is.'

'Like I said, Mr Khan, money isn't my prime motive in life.' I looked over at Melanie.

Khan saw my look. 'You are with a beautiful woman, Mr Sharman. No doubt you wish to return to her side.'

I nodded.

'You look like a man who is used to the company of beautiful women.'

'I've had my moments,' I said.

'I too once had a beautiful woman. Meena's mother. But she is no longer with me. In a way that's for the best. This business would have broken her heart.'

I knew what he was going to say.

'She died three years ago. I'm sure that if she was still with us none of this would have happened.'

'I'm sorry,' I said, and I meant it. 'I'm no stranger to death myself. I've lost many people.'

'Death sits beside all of us, Mr Sharman. It is our constant companion.'

I knew what he meant. And the way he said it made me warm to him slightly. 'I'll have to think about this, Mr Khan,' I said. 'How can I contact you?'

He took a thick business card and a pen from his pocket and wrote an address and number on the back. 'I'm staying at a hotel in Bayswater. I'll be there until Monday morning. Please think about my offer.'

'I will,' I said and rose from the table. 'I'll be in touch.'

Seven

'So what was all that about?' asked Melanie when I got back to our table and lit a cigarette.

'Big trouble in little India.'

'What kind of trouble?'

'The domestic kind. His daughter's done a runner.'

'Why?'

'She met someone and Daddy didn't approve.'

'Why not?'

'Well he's white for a start.'

'What's that got to do with it?'

'Don't be so naive, Mel. A lot. Everything in fact. Why do you think he was getting so aereated?'

'Like that, is he?' she said.

'Very much so. Our Mr Khan seems to think that the entire population of this country are just lazy racist pigs.'

'Maybe he's not far wrong.'

'Maybe not. And she's promised to another.'

'But she's not keen.'

'Never met the fella. It was arranged between the parents.'

She gave Khan a dirty look over her shoulder. 'Does that still go on? Do they go in for female circumcision too? And segregation of women when they're having their periods because they're unclean?'

She was getting a bit aereated herself, and I knew why. It always happened just before her time of the month, and I thought that now wasn't the time to tell her the one about the only difference between a woman with PMT and a Rottweiler was lipstick. I didn't fancy walking home wearing the dregs of her latest Irish coffee down my front. So instead all I said was, 'Now don't start getting political on me.'

She gave me a dirty look too and I knew my decision had been the right one. 'And he wants you to find her?' she asked. 'Is that what it's all about?'

'Correct.'

'Are you going to do it?'

'Dunno. I told him I'd think about it. I don't think so. I

didn't like the man.'

'He was getting pretty excited there for a minute. I thought he was going to take a swing at you.'

'Me too. Or have a heart attack. I told you. He's very old fashioned in his ways. And I rather think he expects a certain amount of deference from his employees.'

'Which you didn't supply.'

'I'm not one of his employees.'

'But you might be.'

'I might be, but right now I'm just an ordinary bloke out enjoying a quiet meal.'

Whilst we'd been speaking Khan had been joined by his two silent companions and then Suri trotted over and they had a little chat before the away team got up and marched out of the restaurant without a glance at us. Suri headed in Mel's and my direction again.

'May I join you?' he asked when he arrived at our table.

'Please do,' I replied.

Suri pulled up an empty chair and sat between us. 'Mr Khan told me he enjoyed your talk. He was most impressed with you.'

'It didn't seem like that to me, and I can't say that I feel the same way,' I said.

Suri's face fell. 'Did he offend you?'

'Not particularly. I've been offended by experts. I just didn't like him. His attitude got up my nose.'

'But are you going to take up his offer of work?'

'I don't know. I told him I'd be in touch. I doubt it somehow.'

'It would be a great personal favour to me if you did.'

'I take it you know what the job is,' I said.

Suri nodded. 'Mr Khan is devastated.'

'His pride's hurt, more like,' I said.

'No. He loves his family and Meena was the apple of his eye.'

'You'd think she was dead the way people talk about her.'

'Mr Sharman. In our culture she might as well be. At least to men like Mr Khan. Some of us are a little more liberal. The younger ones like me. But his generation…' He didn't finish.

'Maybe so,' I said.

'And since his wife died—'

'I know Suri. I got the full half-hour,' I interrupted.

He looked at Mel and me. 'I don't understand,' he said.

'The whole story,' I explained.

'I see. And you felt no compassion.'

'Suri. The man more or less accused me of racism to my face, and my only crime it seemed to me was to come out to dinner, then do you both a favour and listen to his sad little story. And he's the biggest racist of the lot of us. I don't need that kind of shit at the end of a hard week.' I didn't dare look at Melanie as I said the last bit in case she burst out laughing, but I felt justified in a little exaggeration. 'He rubbed me up the wrong way. Sorry, Suri.'

'But this is business, Mr Sharman. Did he not make you a reasonable offer?'

'Very reasonable. He offered to double my fee. But you know—'

'Are you busy?' It was his turn to interrupt.

'No.'

'Then consider the offer, Mr Sharman. Please. I know you are no racist. That's ridiculous. He is upset. He over-compensates. He is a good man in reality. A kind man. You don't know him like I do. Please think about it. For my sake if for no other. '

I gave in. It was easier to do that than to keep arguing. Besides I was fond of Suri and I could tell it was important to him. 'All right Suri,' I said. 'I'll think about it.'

His face split into a white-toothed grin. 'Then we shall have a brandy to celebrate. The best in the house, and I shall take pleasure in tearing up the bill for your dinner.'

So we did and he did.

Eight

MELANIE AND I walked back home together arm in arm after we'd finally finished our meal. We got there around eleven-thirty. I put on the kettle for coffee and she watched me with that kind of look I'd come to know so well from all the women that had ever been in my life from my mother onwards. And believe me there've been plenty. Too many, if you want to know.

'Anything on TV?' I said to deflect it. I knew there was trouble brewing, and I didn't mean in the cafetière.

'Can't you forget the TV for once?'

'Why should I? *TFI Friday*'s on. You know I love Chris Evans. He's such a wag.' Actually I think he's a prick, but I had to have some excuse.

She shook her head sorrowfully.

Christ, I thought. How many times have I been here before?

'Nick,' she said.

I put up my hand like a traffic policeman. 'Don't,' I said. 'Don't say it. Don't even think it.'

'What?'

'The usual. "You're wasting your life." "Think about the future." "Take the job." All the old bollocks. I told you before. I'm not broke. I don't need to work right now. Anyway, I choose what I want to do. What jobs I take, or don't, which-ever the case may be, if you'll excuse the pun. That's what I am. Please don't tell me how to run my life.'

'But Nick…'

'What do you want from me, Melanie?' I asked as I felt the icy grip of reality clutch at my heart. Time after time this has happened. Everything's tickety-boo, and then someone, gener-ally a woman, has to puncture the balloon and let the cold water of truth into my nice comfortable world.

'I don't know,' she replied. 'I thought you'd change.'

'Under your tender ministrations you mean,' I said. 'But if you wanted me to change, what did you see in me in the first place?'

'Someone exciting.'

'But I'm not that exciting, Mel,' I said in exasperation. 'Exciting things just happen round me, don't you see?'

She nodded and came up close so that I could smell her perfume. 'I'm sorry,' she said. 'I just hate to see you wasting your life.'

'But I'm not,' I said, putting my arms on her shoulders and drawing her even closer until I could feel the points of her breasts on my chest and her thighs on mine. 'At least I don't think I am. This is me, babe. I know you hate it when you go off to work and leave me in bed. You think I'm just a lazy bastard, and maybe you're right. But you've got to remember I don't get a pay cheque every month and all the benefits that go with it. I'm walking a tightrope and if I fall there's no safety net. Can you imagine me going off down the DSS and telling them I need the dole. They'd laugh in my face. That's the decision I made years ago and right or wrong, win or lose, that's the deal. I'm too old and ugly to change now. If you can't handle that…' I left the sentence unfinished.

She smiled up at me. 'OK,' she said. 'You're right. I'll mind my own business. It's almost my time of the month. You know what that does to me.'

'I know,' I said.

'Just one thing though.'

'What?'

'The kettle's boiled.'

I made the coffee and poured a couple of brandies and we caught the tail end of Chris Evans' show, but it didn't even make me smile. At twelve-thirty we went to bed and made love, but I could tell it wasn't up to scratch and I guessed that Melanie could too. She fell asleep after, and I lay awake until I got up and sat at what the estate agent long ago called the break-fast bar, but in reality was just a Formica laminated plank of chipboard, and smoked a Silk Cut and thought about my life.

Before I'd stubbed out the cigarette half finished I'd had enough of that, and instead thought about what Khan had told me.

Then I thought about Suri pleading with me after Khan left, and the less than subtle pressure that Melanie was exerting on me to get my life right, and I realised that before the weekend was through I'd probably take the sodding case on.

But then, at least I'd get a decent fuck if I did.

Nine

I WENT BACK to bed and finally fell asleep somewhere in the wee small hours and didn't open my eyes again until ten-ten by the clock on the bedside table. Melanie was curled up in a ball next to me, the short nightie she insisted on wearing rucked up round her waist and her bare bottom pushing into my back. Listen, there are some compensations for being hen-pecked.

I turned round and pulled back the bedclothes. She was dead to the world and I let her be. I got up, tugged on my dressing gown, put on the kettle and went into the bathroom to clean my teeth and take a piss.

I came back and made some tea, sat where I'd sat the night before and lit the first cigarette of the morning.

Melanie isn't the fastest individual when it comes to getting it together in the morning, hence her tiny resentment when she has to get up early for work, but this being Satur-day I just let her lie in. You know, secretly, there's nothing better than having someone trust you that much that they can sleep on whilst you're around.

It was close to eleven before she started to come back to the world and by then I was washed, shaved and dressed and on my third cup.

Eventually she stuck her nose up from under the sheet and said sleepily. 'What day zit?'

'Saturday,' I replied. 'Don't worry. No work.'

'Thank God. Whassa time?'

'Pubs are nearly open,' I replied.

'Trust you.'

'And a very good morning to you too, my love.'

'You're cheerful.'

'I made a decision last night whilst you were dreaming about me.'

'I *thought* I'd had a nightmare.'

'Amusing.'

She sat up and rubbed the sleep out of her eyes. One breast was fully exposed and I grinned.

She looked down, frowned and pushed it safely back under the black silk of her nightie. 'Spoilsport,' I said.

'What kind of decision?'

'Probably the worst kind if past experience is anything to go by. I'll phone Khan. Tell him I'll try and find his daughter for him.'

She grinned through the wisps of hair that fell over her face, pushed back the duvet and gave me an interesting flash of blonde pubic hair as she came off the bed and over to where I was standing. She threw her arms round me and I smelt the warm bed on her and her night-time breath as she hugged me. 'Oh Nick,' she said. 'That's great.'

'How come?' I said, holding her away from me. 'I thought you were a feminist. This girl has run away from an arranged marriage, don't forget.'

'You haven't promised to be best man,' she said pragmatically.

'I haven't promised anything yet,' I said.

'I know. But you will. And if anyone can find her you can. That's the deal, isn't it? You just find her?'

'Yeah. I suppose.'

'So find her, reconcile the family, and let her explain to her father why she had to run away. Take the money he's offering and feel good about yourself.'

'What about all that business of female circumcision and being unclean?'

'I'd had a few last night, Nick.'

'And now all your principles have gone out of the window because you're sober.'

'No. But better you are on the case than anyone else. I've seen what you can do for people.'

'Stop it or I'll start to blush. But it's nice to know you've got faith.'

'I've got faith in you.'

'I hope it's not misguided.'

'It won't be. Just get her back.'

'I get it. And everything in the garden will be lovely, just like that.'

'That's it.'

'I wish I had your belief in human nature, Mel,' I said. 'In my experience things aren't that cut and dried.'

'Well you should have. My belief in human nature, I mean.'

'I don't know. That bloke Khan gave me the willies big time. I don't trust him.'

'What can he do?'

'Don't ask me. Families are funny things.'

'He'll be OK. He just wants his daughter back.'

'We'll see. Now I'm just going to talk to him. I'm not promising anything. It'll probably need a trip to Manchester, and Manchester isn't my favourite town. It's grim up north, love, never forget that.'

'I won't. You'll find his daughter. I know it. And you can buy me a present with all that money you'll earn.'

'I knew there was a hidden agenda,' I said as I kissed her, night-time breath or not. 'I'll make you some tea. Now get yourself together. Half the day's gone and not a penny earned.'

She giggled and headed for the bathroom herself and I gave her a friendly slap on her bottom as she went.

Women. Can't live with them, can't shoot them.

Well not too often anyway.

Ten

I CALLED KHAN whilst Melanie was putting her warpaint on in the bathroom. I got through to his hotel and whoever answered in his room, or suite or whatever, after asking who I was, put his hand over the mouthpiece so's all I could hear was rumbling in my ear as he spoke. Then the line cleared and a voice said. 'Rajesh Khan.'

'Mr Khan,' I said. 'Nick Sharman.'

'Good morning, Mr Sharman. Thank you for calling.'

'I said I would.'

'But not everyone is as good as their word.'

'I am. *When* I give it.'

'That's gratifying to hear. Have you come to a decision?'

'More or less.'

'And?'

'And I think we should meet again. I'll need some details, and copies of those photographs you showed me.'

'You mean you'll take the job?'

I hesitated. Half of me wanted to say no, the other that I would. Then I thought about Suri and Melanie, and how I'd have to explain if I didn't. And the ear bashing I'd have to take. So I blew out a breath and said, 'Yes, Mr Khan.'

'Why? You didn't seem very keen when we met.'

'I wasn't. To be honest I'm still not totally. I'm not sure I agree with arranged marriages.'

'They are a fact of life.'

'I understand that.'

'And I just want my daughter back.'

'I understand that too. I would myself under similar circumstances. That's the main reason why I'm agreeing to take the job on.'

'And the other reasons?'

'I was convinced that I should.'

'May I ask by whom?'

I love people who use the word 'whom'.

'Suri for one. My girlfriend for another. Myself for the third if the truth be known. I've been getting lazy,' I said.

'Excellent. When shall we meet?'

'You're in town until Monday, as I recall.'

'Very early on Monday. I have appointments in Manchester. I'm catching the first plane back that morning.'

'How about tomorrow? I'm busy today, and that means I can start bright and early on Monday morning.'

'Fine. Would noon suit you?'

'That suits me fine.'

'You have the address of the hotel. Just ask for me at the desk.'

'I'll do that. Now you mentioned doubling my usual fee.'

'That's correct. How much do you normally charge?'

'Three hundred a day. Plus expenses. I expect a retainer.'

'I would expect nothing less myself. I imagine you'll accept a cheque.'

'Of course.'

'Would six thousand be sufficient? That should cover you for a week or so.'

'That will do fine,' I replied. Christ, that'd cover me for months but I stayed calm.

'Then noon tomorrow it is.'

'I'll be there.' We made our goodbyes and I put down the phone.

Melanie had reappeared by this time looking alert and ready for anything. 'Was that him?' she asked.

'The very same. I'm seeing him tomorrow.'

'What about today?'

'I told him I was busy today.'

'What sort of busy?'

'I've sort of got plans for us today.'

'What sort of plans?'

'Drinks, lunch, illegal drugs, and an evening screwing.'

She looked at me. 'God, but you're a smooth talking bastard,' she said.

Eleven

WE SAUNTERED DOWN to my local pub and joined the happy throng getting lagered up before rushing home to watch football on Sky TV, then had a few ourselves before lunch at the pizza and pasta emporium next door. Full up to the brim with spaghetti *vongole* and white wine we headed home for the promised late afternoon and evening of carnal delight. The phone was ringing when I opened my flat door and I scooped up the receiver. 'Hello, Dad, it's me.' It was my sixteen-year-old daughter Judith phoning from Scotland.

'Hello sweetie,' I said. 'What's cooking?'

'School work, the usual.'

'You sound so enthusiastic.'

'Not really.' She'd done well in her exams and was in the sixth form studying for her highers.

'Stick at it love, it'll pay off in the end.'

'That's what everybody says.'

'Unfortunately for once everybody's right. You want to go to university, don't you?'

'Suppose so.' Teenage angst, don't you just love it?

'How's your social life?' I asked, changing the subject. 'Got a boyfriend yet?'

'Don't be so predictable, Dad.'

'Well have you?'

'No. It's just me and the girls hanging out together at the moment.'

'Groovy.'

'*Dad*.' She hated it when I used language like that. So I did it all the more to tease her.

'What?' I asked innocently.

'You sound so dated. No one says groovy any more.'

'They do in the places I go.'

'Then you should stay out of places like them.'

We speak a different language now. But I can remember the time when, if I held my daughter close enough, everything in her little world was all right. But that was a long time ago. So long ago that I can barely remember it, and I'm sure she's totally forgotten. And now wasn't the time to remind her. Maybe that time would never come.

'Sorry. I'm suitably chastened,' I said. 'Maybe I should say "cool".'

'Oh Dad.'

'Oh Judith.'

'How's Melanie?' she asked. They'd met and seemed to get on OK.

'Fine. She's here now.'

'That's nice. Are you working?'

Another woman on my case. So what's new? 'Just taking on a job, as a matter of fact,' I said.

'Good. But nothing dangerous, I hope.'

She worries. 'No. Just a missing person,' I said.

'Oh God. You remember the last missing person case you took, don't you?'

I certainly did. 'Don't worry. It's nothing like that. A girl. Just a bit older than you.'

'Well, just be careful.'

'I will.'

'Promise?'

'Course.'

'OK then.' But she didn't sound convinced.

'When shall I see you then?' I asked.

'Christmas I suppose.'

'Don't sound so keen.'

'I won't, don't worry.'

'Until Father Christmas calls, that is.'

'I think I stopped believing in Father Christmas when I was seven years old.'

'Tell that to my credit card company.'

'Listen, Dad I've got to go, I'll talk to you next week.'

'OK honey, take care.'

'You too. Love to Melanie.'

'Course.'

'Bye.' And with that she hung up in my ear.

'Judith?' said Melanie.

'No. My new girlfriend.'

'I suspected as much.'

'Did you indeed?'

'I'd better not or you're in trouble.'

'So tell me something new.'

Melanie put on the kettle for coffee and I rolled a joint of superior grass that I'd scored from some bad boy snow-boarder who hung around the minicab office next to mine. It was pretty powerful stuff and its pungent odour filled the room, mixing with the smell of coffee and all was pretty much right with the world.

Oh yeah. And then I got my reward for being a good boy.

Twelve

THE NEXT MORNING, after a replay of the previous night's lust, I showered Melanie's smell off me, shaved, ate a hearty breakfast and headed for Khan's hotel.

I drove up to town, giving my ancient Ford Mustang a spin. It was a ridiculous motor. Noisy, unreliable and hopeless for surveillance work with a gas-guzzling 5.7 litre V8 engine under the bonnet that was more than half the length of the entire car. But I'd got it off my mate Charlie who'd killed himself that summer and I was damned if I was going to part with it. Christ knows what I was going to do for cars now that he was gone.

It was sitting on the parking space at the front of the house looking like a shark waiting for a tasty morsel to swim by. I started it with a few pumps on the accelerator. It snarled into life, coughed, spat out black smoke and settled down to a lumpy tickover. I selected reverse on the automatic box and it stalled as I knew it would. I started it again, put it back into gear and slammed on the gas. It shot backwards into the street with a yelp from the oversized tyres on the drive wheels and a roar from the cherry bombs fitted to the exhaust that was almost guaranteed to wake anyone in the street having a late Sunday morning lie-in.

I headed up the South Circular and the engine calmed down as it warmed up. I rolled down the window, lit a cigarette and prepared to enjoy the rest of the drive.

I found the hotel in the Bayswater Road and parked round the corner in a residents' bay and went inside.

The receptionist was expecting me and directed me to the lift with instructions to go to the top floor.

It *was* a suite that Khan was staying in. Very nice too, with a view of the main drag and the park beyond. One of his silent henchmen opened the door and gestured for me to enter. The other was sitting at a table by the window. Khan was on the sofa. He got up when I came in and the quiet pair went into another room. 'Chatty, aren't they?' I said.

'They know their place,' said Khan.

'That's something I never learned.'

'I can believe that, Mr Sharman.'

He gestured me to an armchair and sat back on the sofa with a low coffee table between us. 'A drink?' he asked.

'Coffee would be good.'

He picked up the phone that sat on the table, hit a couple of buttons and whispered something into the mouthpiece. 'A moment,' he said.

'Do you mind if I smoke?' I asked.

'Not at all.'

I lit up and seconds later one of the silent ones came in with a tray. He put it on the table and left again. 'Are you going to be mother?' I said.

Khan laughed. 'Your show of contempt for me is admirable.'

'Not contempt, Mr Khan,' I replied. 'It's just my way.'

'So what do you want to know?' he asked when he'd poured me coffee and I was sitting comfortably with an ashtray on the arm of my chair.

'Tell me a little more of the background to all this,' I said. 'You sound like a close family. It must've taken a lot for your daughter to leave.'

'We *are* a close family. Were, at least. Until all this happened. We live in a pleasant suburb. My brothers and sister and their families live nearby. My mother is still alive and lives with my sister and her husband. We always gather together for birthdays and religious festivals. The houses are always full of children. It was a good life. At least until that scum came along.'

'Paul Jeffries,' I interjected.

'Of course Paul Jeffries. We made him so welcome. I cannot believe that we allowed such a snake into our midst.'

'Didn't you realise what was happening? Between him and your daughter, I mean.'

'No. He was clever. The older children, my sons and daughter and their friends of that age, would go around together. The boys were supposed to protect the girls. Some bad things are happening in Manchester. Drugs, guns, gangs. Paul Jeffries was always there, and later I found out he would meet Meena on her own. That was forbidden. As I told you, she was promised to another.'

'A culture clash.'

'Precisely, Mr Sharman. These children scorn the old ways. But the old ways are the best ways. Respect for their elders. Traditional dress. Our language. It is all vanishing. All around I see our way of life being westernised. It must not be allowed to happen.'

'But it's inevitable that it will, Mr Khan,' I said.

'Over my dead body.'

Thirteen

I WAS BEGINNING to understand why Meena had taken it on her toes. This guy was enough to drive anyone out of the house. 'And no one suspected what was going on?'

'Of course not. They were cunning. That is what hurts me most. Not the way he treated our hospitality. But the way he lied and deceived us, and how he turned my daughter against me.'

There were tears in his eyes and all this was getting us nowhere. 'Those photos you showed me,' I said, changing the subject. 'I'd like a set. And Paul Jeffries' mother's and brother's addresses if you have them.'

'No problem. I have made my own enquiries there.'

'Have you seen her? The mum, I mean.'

'She has been visited.'

'And?'

'And nothing. She wasn't cooperative.'

'Did you give her a hard time?'

'I didn't go. My sons saw her.'

'Tough boys or what?'

'They can be.'

'Did they try to put the frighteners on?'

'I don't know. As I said, I wasn't there.'

'But you know.'

'Perhaps they were a little overzealous.'

'That means they did put the frighteners on. I won't. I don't get heavy with old ladies as a rule.'

'She's not that old.'

'And that's an excuse.'

He shook his head.

'How about the brother?'

'He has not been seen.'

'Your boys are OK with old ladies but not with young men. Is that it?'

'No. I stopped them. I didn't want any more trouble.'

'You'll leave that to me, yeah?'

'Perhaps.'

'I'd like to talk to your sons at some point too.'

'Why?'

'Isn't that obvious? They knew Jeffries better than anyone.' Apart from your daughter I thought, but didn't voice what I was thinking. 'Now about Meena's friends,' I said instead. 'The ones that went round with her.'

'What about them?'

'Someone knows something. I know young girls. They love to talk. She's told someone something. Do you know them?'

He shrugged. 'Girls would come to the house. They would lock themselves away with sticky drinks and sweets and play their awful music. They were like so many brightly coloured birds.'

'And your sons chaperoned them, when they went to town.'

'Sometimes. Sometimes it was members of the girls' families. They took it in turns.'

'I might have to come up to Manchester. Snoop around a bit.'

'Do you think that's really necessary?'

'I don't know. Maybe, maybe not. If I happen to bump into Meena and Paul coming out of Tesco's probably not. But if they've made it difficult enough for you and your network to come up with nothing, then any information would be useful.'

'I see. Well if it is necessary I will arrange accommodation.'

'I'll hold you to that. But introductions would be more important. I'm sure that the girls' parents wouldn't thank some middle-aged white man for scaring them half to death. We'd have to be careful.'

'I agree.'

'That can come later. First off I'll see Mum and try and reason with her. The boy's been in jail, you say. Maybe I can suggest that it might be better for him to talk to me than go back.'

'I said no police.'

'His mother doesn't know that.'

'True.'

'And if she's no help I'll track down the brother.'

'Whatever you need to do to bring Meena home.'

'Meanwhile I trust you'll keep looking yourself.'

'Of course.'

'That's good. Now the photos, please.'

He took out the same envelope as he'd carried on the previous Friday and took out the two photos again. 'The one of Meena is a copy. Of Jeffries the original.'

'I'll take care of them,' I said.

He took a small address book and a silver pen from his inside pocket, referred to a page and wrote something on the back of the envelope. 'Mrs Jeffries' address,' he explained. 'It is in a place called Norbury. Are you familiar with that?'

'I know Norbury,' I said.

He wrote more. 'And the brother, Peter Jeffries. An address in Croydon.'

'Handy. It's just down the road from Norbury.'

'And your fee.'

'Please.'

He took a company-sized cheque book from the same pocket, opened it and said, 'I believe the figure mentioned was six thousand.'

'That's right.'

He wrote out the cheque carefully and signed it. 'I'm glad you agreed to take the job,' he said when he handed it over.

I folded the thick paper and popped it into my pocket with the envelope containing the photos and addresses. 'Me too, Mr Khan,' I said although I wasn't sure that I was. This whole thing looked like a minefield. Families always are. 'I assume I can reach you on the numbers on the card you gave me.'

'Night or day. The first number is my office, the second my home, or use the mobile. It's always switched on.'

'Then that's it,' I said. 'I'll get on this first thing tomorrow.'

He rose too and we shook hands.'Good luck, Mr Sharman,' he said.

'Thank you,' I replied, and I reckoned I was going to need it.

Fourteen

WHEN I GOT home Melanie was watching the *EastEnders* omnibus on TV. I walked in and dropped my jacket on the arm of the sofa and sat next to her. 'How did it go?' she asked as she killed the volume.

'Great,' I replied, lighting a Silk Cut. 'Just terrific. Wonderful. I'm not surprised young Meena split. That Khan geezer is a pain in the arse big time. A real prince among men, I don't think. If I was related to him I'd've left years ago.'

'As bad as that?'

'Worse.'

'Poor Nicky, was the big man howwible?' She put on a little girl voice.

'Don't,' I said, trying hard not to laugh and not succeeding.

'But you took the job.'

'I took the job. For a week or so. On approval if you like.'

'Did he pay you?'

'You're a mercenary little sod, do you know that?' I said.

'I work in the City. I'm paid to be mercenary.'

'He gave me a cheque,' I said.

'Show me.'

I took out the piece of paper and dropped it in her lap. 'Six grand,' she said. 'For a *week*. Do you know how long it takes me to earn six grand?'

'Or *so*. A week or *so*,' I reminded her. 'And no I don't know how long it takes you to earn six grand.'

'A bloody long time.'

'My heart bleeds.'

'Do you think it'll bounce?'

'It better not. Or maybe it'd be better if it did. Then I could just forget the whole thing.'

'Don't be like that, Nick.'

'I feel like being like that.'

'So what are you going to buy me?' she asked ingenuously.

'I don't know. How about some sexy underwear?'

'You men are all alike. You think us woman are turned on by stiff bits of lace that always work themselves up into our backsides and feel like you're wearing an elastic band up your jacksie.'

'Most of you are turned on by stiff somethings anyway,' I remarked.

'You're disgusting.'

'That wasn't what you said when I was talking dirty to you this morning.'

At least she had the grace to blush.

I opened a bottle of red wine and poured us each a glass and joined her on the couch as a bunch of ugly actors from RADA silently mouthed some idiot's idea of what went on in an East End pub like goldfish on the screen. Have you ever been in an East End boozer where no one uses the F-word and no one ever makes a racist remark? I haven't.

'Have you got photos of the missing pair?' Melanie asked when she'd had a sip of her wine.

I took the photos out of the envelope and showed her. 'She's beautiful,' she said when she'd given them a scan. 'He looks like a right Jack the lad.'

'That's probably the attraction,' I observed. 'I think she was on a short rein at home.'

'Women always seem to go for bad boys.'

'Is that why you go for me?'

'Who says I do?'

'You're here, aren't you?'

'Pig.'

We spent the rest of the afternoon finishing off the bottle and fooling around on the sofa. It was good to have someone around who cared about me and who I cared about.

I put the Khan family problems out of my mind. There'd be plenty of time for them in the morning when I'd have to go out and start earning his bloody six thousand quid.

Fifteen

T HE NEXT MORNING after Melanie had gone to work I went to work too. I left it until eleven o'clock to drive to Norbury and hunt out Paul Jeffries' mother. I'm a great believer in letting the streets air before I venture forth.

I dug out my A-Z and looked up the street where she lived. It was bang in the middle of that conurbation of suburban streets between Streatham and Croydon where I'd spent a great part of my adolescence searching for sex and drugs and rock and roll, and occasionally finding all three. But mostly not.

I drove down in the Mustang and parked it two streets away and took a stroll. It's good to familiarise yourself with where people live before talking to them, and besides it was a trip back in time for me.

It didn't seem to have changed much from when I shlepped around in pursuit of illicit pleasures, but like anywhere and anyone else it must've done, and I wondered what the young and innocent boy who thought he knew so much would have made of the middle-aged man I was now, who'd finally come to realise he knew almost nothing. Not a lot, I'd imagine.

The street itself was in the shadow of the twin television masts on the hills above Norbury, short, crammed with higgledy-piggledy terraced houses, some that had been renovated and some left as they must have looked when they were built a century or more before. On one corner was a little grocery, on the other a baker's, with a launderette next door and an MOT specialist garage down the narrow alleyway between. Both sides of the street were lined with parked cars and it was so typically south London it almost hurt.

The number I was looking for was about halfway down on the right. The house had been painted deep pink at one time but the paint was faded and peeling although some effort had been made to keep the tiny front garden tidy, and the front gate was in one piece.

I opened it and walked up the path to the front door through the autumn sunshine and the chilly wind that blew litter behind me and knocked.

The woman who answered it a few moments later was in her late fifties with dark hair shot with grey and wearing a cardigan over a blouse and skirt. 'Mrs Jeffries,' I asked pleasantly.

'That's right. If it's about the council tax again, I've sent a letter to—'

'It's not about the council tax, Mrs Jeffries,' I interrupted. 'It's about your son Paul.'

Her face hardened. 'Are you the police?'

I shook my head. 'No,' I replied. 'I'm a private enquiry agent. My name's Sharman. Nick Sharman. A Mr Khan has asked me to help him find his daughter Meena.'

Her face hardened even more at that. 'If you've come here to harass me again—'

'No harassment Mrs Jeffries, I can assure you.' I interrupted again. 'I'm just trying to find Meena Khan. Her father believes she's with Paul. All I want to do is to get in touch with them. Mr Khan's very upset. A few questions, that's all.'

'Is that why he sent those sons of his to break down my door?'

'I don't know anything about that, Mrs Jeffries,' I went on, fearing that I was losing control of the situation. I'd guessed that Khan's boys had got out of order, but I wasn't sure by how much. 'I just want five minutes of your time.'

She looked at me closely and I could see her deciding whether to cut me off or not, so I gave her what I hoped was a charming smile. It seemed to work. 'All right then,' she said, 'I suppose you'd better come in. You are alone?' She looked up and down the street as if expecting a posse of Indians to be hiding under a parked car.

'Yes,' I said. 'I work alone.'

'Come on then.' And she opened the door all the way and stepped back.

I went inside, closed the door behind me and she led me down a narrow hall to a tiny sitting room with kitchen attached, overlooking a postage stamp sized back garden where the remains of the summer flowers still bloomed. On the mantelpiece there was a picture of Paul in a suit with another young man standing beside him. It looked like it had been taken at a wedding or similar family function. Next to it was a photograph of another youngster with a strong family resemblance. I guessed it was brother Peter.

'Sit down,' said Mrs Jeffries and indicated an armchair by the cold fireplace next to a bookcase overflowing with Mills & Boon titles. Thin and sexless they are. My mind turned to Melanie who was exactly the opposite. Curvy and sexy.

'Cup of tea?'

I was stung from my reverie. 'Love one,' I said as I took the chair and she filled the kettle from the tap and plugged it in.

There was an awkward silence and I thought that I was losing it again when we were interrupted by the appearance of a huge marmalade cat who sashayed over and jumped up into my lap. 'Marmaduke,' she said to the cat. 'Don't do that.' Then to me. 'Just push him off if he's a nuisance.'

'No worries,' I said. 'I like cats,' and I petted the animal under the chin until he started purring.

The comfortable scene seemed to make Mrs Jeffries feel better and she began to relax. 'I don't know where Paul is,' she said as she prepared the tea things.

'Has he been in touch recently?' I asked.

'Not for weeks.'

'But since he went off with Meena?'

She thought about that for a minute before nodding.

'Where was he, do you know?'

'If I did I wouldn't tell you. Those boys who came scared me.'

'I'm sorry about that,' I said. 'And I'm sorry about your door and any damage they did. I'm sure Mr Khan would be happy to pay.'

'He already did. I threatened him with the law. He didn't like that.'

So much for Khan not knowing what had gone on.

'I think the family was just upset about Paul and Meena running away like they did.'

'Well, wouldn't you?' she said.

'Wouldn't I what?'

'Run away if someone threatened to kill you.'

Sixteen

'Come again,' I said, astonished.
'They threatened to kill Paul and Meena.'

'Khan's *sons* did? Her *brothers*.'

'And Khan himself. That was the message they brought from him. You don't understand what a terrible thing Meena did by running away with Paul. To people of their religion, that was the ultimate betrayal.'

'And how about you?' I asked. 'How do you feel about it?'

'Not betrayed if that's what you mean. I always wanted Paul to settle down. Get married to a nice girl and have some babies maybe. I just wish it wasn't under these kinds of circumstances.'

'So you'd have them here?'

'Like a shot.'

'That's good,' I said thoughtfully.

'You don't believe me, do you?' she said. 'I can see it by the look on your face. But it's true. Take my word.'

'I just don't believe a father threatening to kill his own child.' I thought of Judith and the joke I'd made about boyfriends. I knew it was going to be tough when she finally got one, but I thought I'd stop short of making death threats. 'I've got a child of my own about Meena's age. I could never see me doing that, whatever she did.'

'Believe it. Paul and Meena are terrified. That's why they keep running. And I've got those people watching me all day long.'

'What people?' I sensed paranoia here. But always remember that just because you're paranoid doesn't mean they aren't out to get you. I've been paranoid in my time and it's saved my life more than once.

'The people in the corner shop,' she explained. 'Indians. Mr Patel and his family. That's why Paul and Meena could never come here.'

I remembered what Khan had said about his network. 'Then why did you let me in?' I asked.

'What?'

'When I told you I was working for the Khans. Why let me in here if you think they're potential killers? Presumably that makes me one as well.'

'Because you're a white man, Mr Sharman. And I can talk to you. You have a nice face. And I'm at the end of my tether. Sometimes I think I'd be better off dead anyway. I'm not frightened any more. I want you to go back to them and tell them to stop all this. You can do that, can't you?'

'I don't think I have that kind of power.'

'Just try.'

'It's not because you're frightened that Paul may end up back inside?'

'You know about that.'

'A little.'

'It was nothing really. Childhood pranks.'

'A bit of burglary, car theft, ABH and drugs. A little more than childhood pranks, I think.'

'He was going straight. Working.'

'Casual.'

'As you so rightly say, Mr Sharman, he has a record. There's more people than jobs out there or hadn't you noticed? But he was trying.'

'Mr Khan is more of the opinion that he wheedled his way in with the family to get to Meena.'

'What can I say then? If you don't believe me you don't believe me. He loves Meena and Meena loves him. They just want a life together. Children. A place to live.'

'I didn't say I didn't believe you, Mrs Jeffries,' I said. 'I know people. I've been lied to by the people who've hired me before. I'll just have to make some further enquiries.'

'Then I suggest you do that.'

'I will,' I answered and sipped at my cool tea. 'Who's that with Paul?' I asked, pointing at the photo of her son and his companion.

She smiled. 'That's Henry. Paul's best friend. They've known each other since primary school. That was taken at Henry's brother's wedding a couple of years ago.'

'Does Henry live round here?'

'Streatham.'

'Do you think he's heard from Paul?'

She gave me a slitty eyed look. 'I have no idea. I haven't

asked. I don't want to involve anyone else.'

'Does he know about what's happened?'

'He knows. He phones me from time to time.'

'Do you have a number for him?'

'I don't want you bothering him.'

'*I'm* not in the habit of breaking doors down, Mrs Jeffries,' I said. 'I just want to talk. Here.' I handed her one of my cards. 'My office and home numbers are both on there. Ask him to give me a call. Just to talk. Nothing else.'

She said nothing as she dropped the card on the table.

'And you too if you want to,' I added. 'Just call me. And I will promise you this. You won't be hassled by anyone from Khan's family or associates again. I'll guarantee that now.' I liked Mrs Jeffries, she reminded me of my own mother. She was just someone trying to get along and didn't deserve this mess. 'Is that your other son?' I asked, pointing at the photograph of the other young man.

'You know a lot,' she said.

'Not really.'

'Yes, that's Peter. He wanted to kill Khan's sons for what they did here. I had to beg him not to. Be careful if you see him, Mr Sharman. He has a short temper.'

'I'll remember that.'

'God knows what he'd do if he knew the Patels were watching me.'

'You haven't told him.'

She shook her head. 'I just want a bit of peace. I'm not as young as I used to be. I don't want any trouble.'

'I'll try to see that you don't get it,' I said.

'Thank you.'

I left her then and walked back up the street and into the grocer's shop. It was empty except for one middle-aged Indian man and a big Alsatian dog that growled softly as I entered.

I took out another of my cards as I approached the counter. 'My name's Sharman,' I said as I dropped the card on top.

'Are you a rep?' the man asked. 'We don't need anything.'

'No,' I replied. 'I work for Rajesh Khan from Manchester. I think you know him.'

The man's dark skin paled slightly and I knew he did.

'No,' he said and touched the dog gently on the head. The dog growled again, a little louder this time.

'I think you do. There's a lady lives down the road in the pink house, number forty. Mrs Jeffries. I want you to leave her alone. Stop spying on her. She's never done you any harm. Tell Mr Khan I said so. I will when I speak to him.'

'I don't know what you're saying,' the man protested. 'You're crazy. Go away or I'll call the police.'

'Call them,' I said. 'There's laws against harassment in this country and you're breaking them.'

'I'll set the dog on you unless you go.'

'Don't threaten me, son,' I said. 'Or I'll tear your fucking dog's throat out and feed it to you, fur and all.'

He jumped to his feet. 'Go!' he screamed and the dog started barking and strained at the leash the man was holding.

'I'm going,' I said.

'And good riddance.'

'Remember what I said. Just tell Mr Khan.' I turned on my heel and went back out into the street.

Seventeen

I WENT BACK to the car and headed back towards Streatham. But as it was still early, and I needed to think, I didn't take my turning home off the South Circular. Instead I let the car take me on through Dulwich and New Cross, out to Greenwich and the cemetery where my second wife, Dawn, our baby Daisy, and our friend Tracey were buried. I left the Mustang in the car park, bought a bunch of flowers from the stall by the gates and walked up the hill where their graves sat overlooking the River Thames and the Isle of Dogs beyond. It was cold and the river was running fast and the place was deserted.

I turned up my collar to the chill breeze, put the flowers between the graves and hunkered down beside them. 'Hello girls,' I said. 'How are you today?'

I pulled some weeds that had pushed through the earth and tossed them on to the grass next to the graves. 'Good,' I said as if they'd answered. 'Me? I'm all right too.'

I hadn't been to the cemetery for a long time. Too long. Since before I'd met Melanie. 'I'm not being unfaithful to you,' I said to Dawn. 'It's just that I get so lonely without you. I need someone to talk to. It takes away the pain. I'll always love you, darling, I'll always love all three of you.'

And I knew that I would. Until the day that I died and was buried next to them up here where the wind blew hard from Russia and we could look at the river together for eternity.

'I've got a case, Dawn,' I said. 'And I think it's more complicated than it seemed. I get a feeling someone's telling me porkies. If you were here you could help me work it out. Remember how you liked playing detective?'

But of course there was no reply and there never would be. Not really. Only in my head, which was the only place that mattered and I could talk to my three girls whenever I wanted to.

The clouds were moving fast in the big sky above me and the sun came and went and the temperature was falling. I stood up and lit a cigarette and shivered as the breeze took the smoke from my mouth. 'I'll come again soon,' I said to them. 'I promise. I'll never forget you and I'll never stop missing you.'

A boat passed by and whoever was standing on the deck waved in my direction. I waved back. 'Wave to them, Daisy,' I said to the daughter I'd never met who'd died inside her mother's womb. 'Wave to them, sweetheart.' And I felt tears prick at my eyes as I walked back to the car with my hands in my pockets and drove home.

Eighteen

W HEN I GOT back to the flat there was a message from Melanie on the ansaphone. I tapped out her work number, got put through to her extension and she answered, 'Melanie Wiltse.'

'Hello sweetheart,' I said. 'What's up?'

'Nothing much here. Usual crap. You know. Whose turn to buy the coffee. You're lucky you don't work with other people. How was your day? Been busy?'

'I went to see Paul Jeffries' mum. She's a nice woman. Been getting hassle from Khan's sons. They busted down her door and threatened everyone including the cat, from what I can gather. And her house is being watched. By the local grocer if you can believe that. Looks like there's more to all this than meets the eye.'

'How?'

'I'll tell you when I see you. How about dinner tomorrow?'

'OK. But I have to get some sleep. I can't concentrate with a hangover.'

Christ! I can't concentrate *without* one these days, I thought. 'I'll get you home by midnight Cinderella, I promise,' I said.

'What are you going to do next?'

'Pour a drink.'

'No. I mean on the case, stupid.'

'Speak to Khan. Find out why he's telling me lies. And I reckon I'll have to go to Manchester soon, though I don't fancy it much. All this started there. And there's bound to be people up there who know what's going on. I'll just have to try and find them.'

'When are you going?'

'I thought about the weekend, maybe sooner.'

'Can I come?'

I was surprised. 'Do you want to?' I asked.

'It'll be a break.'

'A bore, more like. Wandering the streets of a strange town looking for people who might not exist. And in a strange community which won't exactly welcome my questions with open arms.'

'So you could use some company.'

'Suppose so.'

'Don't sound so keen.'

'Those sons of his sound a bit heavy. I don't want to put you into harm's way.' I thought about Dawn and Tracey and Daisy again. That's what I'd done to them. Put them into harm's way and they'd ended up dead. I didn't want any more deaths on my conscience.

'I'll play the little woman. Stay in the hotel and catch up on my knitting,' said Melanie.

'That doesn't sound like you, Mel.'

'I'll try. Or maybe I'll just go out shopping.'

'That sounds more like it.'

'So can I come?'

'OK sweetheart. If you're up for it. I'll speak to Khan later. He did say he'd show me round. But I don't know.'

'What?'

'Whether his idea of showing me round is just showing me what he wants me to see.'

'You'll manage. You always do.'

'I'm glad you're so confident in my abilities.'

'Course I am.'

'OK then, babe. We'll talk about it over dinner. I'll pick you up after work tomorrow. Round about six.'

'I'll look forward to it.'

'Me too. Now take care and I'll see you then.'

'See you.'

I hung up and poured the promised drink, lit a cigarette, slumped down on the sofa and waited for the evening when I'd give my principal a call.

Nineteen

I WAITED UNTIL seven to phone Khan. I punched his home number into the phone and after three rings a woman answered. 'May I speak with Mr Rajesh Khan, please?' I asked politely.

'Mr Khan is just sitting down to dinner,' she replied.

'This won't take long, it's just a small piece of business.'

'He prefers to conduct his business during office hours.'

'This is personal business. About his daughter Meena.'

I heard her catch her breath. 'May I enquire who is calling?' she asked.

'My name is Sharman. Nick Sharman.'

'I will see if he will speak to you.'

How kind, I thought.

She put the phone down with a clunk and I heard voices, then Khan came on. 'Mr Sharman,' he said.

'Sorry to interrupt your meal,' I said.

'That is of no consequence. Jyoti is very protective.'

'Jyoti?' I said.

'Our housekeeper. She has looked after us since my wife died.'

'Right. I spoke to Paul Jeffries' mother today.'

'And?'

'And your sons have been giving her a hard time.'

'That was a mistake. You know what young men are like. Impulsive.'

'Impulsive enough to threaten to kill Paul and Meena. Boys will be boys, is that it?'

'Is that what she said?'

'Yes.'

'Nonsense.'

'I'm not so sure, Mr Khan. She seemed like a decent woman, if scared half to death.'

'I think you exaggerate.'

'About her decency, or your sons' threats?'

'The threats, of course.'

'I don't think so, Mr Khan. And there's a bloke called Patel runs a little shop on the corner of her street. Is it true that you're having him watch her?'

'Hardly. It happens that I know Patel's brother-in-law. I may have mentioned something…'

'Part of your network that stretches far and wide?'

'Precisely.'

'Paul and Meena won't come calling while he's watching.'

'She's heard from them then?'

'Yes. It's amazing what a few gentle questions will get out of people that breaking down their doors doesn't.'

'I told you, my boys are impulsive.'

'Stupid I'd call it.'

He didn't reply.

'Mr Khan,' I said. 'I don't like being lied to. And I don't like people who threaten defenceless women. That has to stop, or else I send you back the money you gave me less one day's fee, and I quit this job. Do you get me?'

He was silent for a moment then he said, 'Yes.'

'And call Patel off. I've already told him what will happen if you don't.'

'What?'

'Something to do with feeding him certain parts of his dog's anatomy.'

'And you call my sons impulsive.' I thought I almost heard amusement in his voice, but I might've been wrong. Probably was.

'So will you tell him? I don't know if he'll listen to me, and I don't want to have to go back.'

'Very well.'

'Good. We're beginning to understand one another.'

'Does Mrs Jeffries know where Paul and Meena are?'

'I don't think so. She obviously believes it's safer if she doesn't. And even if she does, she obviously isn't going to tell me.'

'So what will you do next?'

'Go and find Paul's brother. I hope you haven't set the hounds on him too.'

'No. I've already told you that.'

But you don't always tell me the truth do you? I thought, but once again didn't say it. 'Just old ladies, eh?' I did say. 'Obviously your sons aren't that impulsive. I'd like to meet them. I think I need to come up to Manchester. I'd like to talk to Meena's friends. Somebody up there knows where she is.'

'You think so.'

'I know so.'

'When were you thinking of coming?'

'Towards the end of the week. Thursday, maybe. During the day. By train.'

'I'll book you into a hotel. I can get a deal.'

I never doubted it for a moment. 'Something in the city centre,' I said. 'Decent,' I added.

'I wouldn't put you in anything less.'

'I'm glad to hear it. And I'll need a double room.'

'A *double*.'

'I'm bringing my trusty assistant.'

'I thought you worked alone.'

'Not always.'

'I see.'

'Don't worry, Mr Khan, I'll pay her fare. You'll ring me with details of the hotel?'

'Of course. We can have dinner on Thursday evening. You can bring me up to date with your progress.'

'Sounds good. So I'll see you on Thursday.'

'You will.'

'And Mr Khan.'

'Yes.'

'Let me handle this from now on. That's what you're paying me for.'

'I will, Mr Sharman.'

'And Mr Khan. One last thing.'

'Yes.'

'Enjoy your dinner.' And with that I put down the phone.

Twenty

BRIGHT AND EARLY Tuesday morning I set off to find Paul Jeffries' brother Peter. I went to the address Khan had given to me. It was in a tower block on a reasonable looking estate just outside Croydon. I was lucky all these punters lived in south London. The flat was on the fifteenth floor, but the lift was working so that was OK, and I rang the bell at exactly nine-fifteen by my trusty Rolex.

It was answered by a plump blonde with black roots, a short skirt, leggings, and a Crystal Palace FC sweatshirt. She was carrying a baby in her arms and a toddler peered at me from between her legs like he was worried I'd come for the rent. 'Mrs Jeffries?' I said with a query.

'I'm not married,' she replied with a sort of half scowl.

Sure, I thought, have a couple of kids but don't make any commitment. That's the millennium way. 'Sorry,' I said. 'Does Peter Jeffries live here?'

'Who's asking?' Everyone was so suspicious these days.

'My name's Sharman. It's about his brother.'

She snorted through her nose. 'What's he done now?'

'Nothing really.'

'*Sure.*'

'Does Mr Jeffries live here?' I asked again.

'Yep.'

'Is he at home?'

'Nope.'

'Do you know where he is?'

'At work.'

'Where's that?'

'On the new flyover.' She jerked one hand at the view across Croydon Town and the South Downs beyond. 'New Addington.'

'I know it,' I said.

'Good. Then you won't need to bother us any more,' and she turned and slammed the door in my face. The last thing I saw was the solemn expression on the toddler's face. Good luck, son, I thought. You're going to need it.

I went back to the car and followed the signs for New
Addington, until I came to a line of cars stopped at temporary
lights beside a deep scar in the ground behind a wire fence
that was covered with notices apologising for any delay to
motorists, from the construction company that couldn't care
less if you were stuck in a traffic jam until Doomsday.

I followed the arrows for Site Traffic across an ocean of
muddy clay and parked behind a skip lorry. I got out and
picked my way through the slurry past yet another sign
designating the site as a hard hat area. Deciding to take my
chances against being brained by low-flying earth-moving
equipment I headed for a pale green Portakabin wearing a
handwritten notice that read: SITE OFFICE.

There were two young geezers lolling about outside
drinking something from thick china mugs, both I noted
wearing hard hats. One in acid yellow, the other a fetching
pale blue. 'Morning,' I said as I slid to a halt in the mud.

Neither replied.

Good start, I thought. 'I'm looking for Peter Jeffries,' I said.

'Who wants him?' said Yellow Hat.

'My name's Sharman.' I was getting tired of introducing
myself. 'I'm a private investigator.'

'Blimey,' said Blue Hat. 'Just like on the telly.'

'Not quite,' I replied. 'Is Mr Jeffries about? I won't keep
him long. I just want a word.'

'About what?' asked Blue Hat.

'Is he here?' I was getting tired of these two wankers.

'Might be,' said Yellow Hat. 'What's it about? Has he come
into money?'

'It's private,' I said. 'That's why they call me a private
investigator.'

'Blimey,' said Blue Hat. 'Sounds serious.'

'Not really.'

Blue Hat rapped on the door of the Portakabin with his
knuckles and shouted. 'Pete. You've got a visitor.'

After a moment the door opened and an older version of
the face in the photo on Mrs Jeffries' mantelpiece stuck his
red, hard-hatted head round the corner. 'What?' he demanded.
'I'm on me break.'

'Mr Jeffries,' I said. 'My name's Sharman. I'm looking for
your brother.'

Jeffries smiled an ugly smile and slid between door and jamb. In his hand he was carrying a ball-peen hammer. 'Is that right?' he said. 'You're the cunt who was bothering my mum yesterday, aren't you? I was half expecting you. You've got a fucking cheek. I'm going to teach you a lesson, mate. You'll wish you'd never been born.'

Oh fuck, I thought. Why me?

Twenty-one

THE FIGHT WAS similar to the way I've heard some people's sex lives described – nasty, brutal and short. It should've been easy for them. The odds were stacked against me. There were three of them to my one, they were wearing protective headgear and heavy boots and one was armed. I was wearing soft shoes that slid on the muddy surface of the site, and I've still got one bad foot, even though I often forget about it.

But there were two problems for my assailants. One: they were too confident that they could take me, and two: I was determined not to be drinking my lunch through a straw in the Mayday Hospital for the next month, or worse, dead and buried inside a ton of concrete at the base of the New Addington flyover.

And they should've come in mob handed, but instead like the little gentlemen they were, they let Peter Jeffries make the first move. I half expected that. After all it was his fight and he had the hammer.

And he was going to hammer in the morning, hammer in the evening, all over this land.

He was a silly boy if he believed that.

He raised the tool and swung it at my head hard enough to put a round dent in my skull and finish the whole thing before it had even started.

No such luck Pete, I thought as the heavy hammer whistled through the air and came close enough to ruffle my hair as I pulled my head back, let the weight of the tool pull him slightly off balance as I folded the fingers of my right hand back into my palm and straight-armed him under his chin with my knuckles.

I saw his eyes bulge and he choked on his Adam's apple, dropped the hammer and put both hands up to his throat.

I scooped up the ball-peen and threw it hard at Blue Hat. I didn't like his style. It hit him head first with a thud on his right shoulder and I imagined gave him food for thought and a dead arm.

'Fuck,' he said in pain and grabbed at his shoulder as Yellow Hat charged me like an enraged bull and got me one good one on the side of the head with a left hook that made the world go out of focus.

I stumbled to one side, saw his other fist coming round in a haymaker, stuck up my left arm to deflect the blow and hit him hard in the sternum with my right: that took the wind out of his sails and deposited him on the ground. Blue Hat meanwhile got back into the fray and aimed a kick at my balls which, if it had hit the intended target would have finished me off. But I was lucky: as I turned away from him to avoid his foot, my shoe skidded in the muck and I went down on to my knee and the kick caught me on the shoulder. I rolled back, came up, caught his foot and tugged hard. He went down on top of Yellow Hat who was struggling to his feet, and was knocked down flat on his back again in a mess of arms and legs.

I stood and grabbed Peter Jeffries and slammed him back against the wall of the Portakabin hard enough to shake the structure, knocked off his helmet, grabbed him by his hair and said, 'Stop it now Peter or I'll fucking do you.'

His face was almost as red as his hard hat and he struggled both for breath and to speak. 'I never did anything to your mum,' I hissed. 'Now you can believe that or not but it's true. All I wanted was a friendly chat about your brother and his girlfriend. Do you know where they are?'

Out of the corner of my eye I saw Blue and Yellow Hat stand up. 'Stay back, boys,' I said. 'Or I'll do your mate serious damage. Tell 'em, Peter.'

He lifted one hand palm outwards and they stepped back. 'Good,' I said. Then to Peter, 'Well, do you?'

'No,' he managed to choke out of his bruised throat.

'Are you telling me the truth?' I demanded.

He nodded furiously.

'See,' I said. 'That was it. I'm leaving now, but I may be back. Next time listen before you get stupid. Understand?'

He coughed and spluttered and nodded again. I let go of his hair and skated back to my car through the mud and took off fast before his pals decided to get back into the bundle. I didn't think I'd be so lucky twice. When I was far enough away to know I wasn't being pursued I pulled the car into a side street, lit a cigarette with trembling hands whose trembling gradually spread to the rest of my body and sat shaking for a good five minutes.

Twenty-two

WHEN I'D CALMED down enough to drive, I started the engine and went home. I felt sore all over, and my clothes and the driver's seat of the car were covered in mud. A delightful way to spend a Tuesday morning.

I parked the motor up and limped into the house, dropped my leather jacket on the landing outside my flat door so it wouldn't get the furniture inside all muddy, and once inside stripped down and put the rest of my clothes into the washing machine and switched it on.

Then I went into the shower and stood under water just hot enough to bear before I checked myself in the mirror.

I cleared the condensation off the glass, pushed my hair out of my eyes and winced at my reflection. The right side of my face was swollen up nicely and the first signs of bruising were beginning to appear. I moved my jaw from side to side and it hurt like hell, but I could tell nothing was broken. There were more bruises coming up on my right shoulder and it was tender to touch. But once again no bones broken. My right knuckles were swollen too, and my foot and leg were aching from where I'd slipped. But it could've been worse. A lot worse. I could've been dead.

I dried off and dressed in fresh underwear, shirt, socks and jeans, surveyed the wreckage of my shoes that were pretty well past saving and put them into the trash bag. Then I went outside and rescued my leather jacket, which would be fine once the mud was washed off, and sat down with a cigarette and large Jack Daniel's and considered what had happened.

I'd been pretty stupid and it was more luck than judgement that I'd managed to make it home on my own two feet, or one a half more like.

I sat there for the rest of the afternoon until it was time to go and meet Melanie. I was in no mood to continue the investigation, only in jacking it in pronto. If it hadn't been for the ear bending I'd get from her I would've done it too. But when a woman like her was around, valour was often the better part of discretion.

I put on a suit and tie to go out, and when I checked myself in the mirror again, one half of my face looked like an overripe melon that had taken a good kicking.

Delightful.

I got a cab up to Blackfriars. She was waiting for me in the reception area of her building when I limped in.

'What have you done now?' was the first thing she said when she saw me. If I'd been expecting sympathy I could obviously go on expecting it.

'I went to see Jeffries' brother,' I explained.

'He was obviously pleased to see you.'

'You could say that. Him and his mates.'

'Lots of them, were there?'

'Enough.'

'Christ. Did you ever consider you were in the wrong job? Every time you take on a case you end up in Casualty.'

'And whose idea was it that I took it on in the first place?'

'Don't blame me.'

'Christ, Mel. Do me a favour. I'm stiff all over.'

'*All* over? Maybe my luck's changing.'

'What's happened to women in the nineties?' I said. 'Where's the compassion? The sweetness and light?'

'You want me to mop your fevered brow, is that it?'

'I don't need aggro, that's for sure.'

'Diddums.'

I just sighed. I wasn't going to win and that was that.

We walked up to a tiny Javanese restaurant we'd discovered on Holborn Viaduct. Or at least she walked and I limped along beside her.

The food was good and I told her the story of my day as we ate. She was a bit kinder after that, but not much.

When I'd paid the bill we cabbed over to Gerry's club in Dean Street for a drink, but I was feeling lousy by then. A bit of delayed shock, I reckoned. More like a dodgy prawn in the fish curry, she thought.

We caught another cab back to mine and we were tucked up in bed by eleven-thirty, and if she thought I was going to do all sorts of macho things to her she was very much mistaken.

There's only so much a man can take in one day.

Twenty-three

B UT OF COURSE I couldn't sleep. My face and shoulder hurt like hell and I kept thinking about the Khan case. Melanie, on the other hand, was asleep in minutes whilst I tossed and turned next to her. Eventually, to avoid disturbing her I got up again.

I switched on the weak light that sits on top of my television set and hunted for my cigarettes. I lit one and went and stood by the window looking out into the dark and deserted street outside, massaging my bruises and wincing at the pain I felt from them.

It had started raining on the way home in the cab, the sound of the tyres splashing through puddles and hissing on the wet tarmac almost drowned by the throb of the diesel engine and some fools nattering on the radio in the front.

It was still raining as I stood there, the drops on the window pane outside rolling down like tears and making the glass into a mirror so that I could see Melanie lying in bed behind me. The distortion of the rain and the blackness of the sky outside changed the colour of her skin in the dim light from the lamp and for a moment I imagined she was dead lying there, and I shivered as I thought about what Khan had said about death – it being our constant companion. And of course he was right. As the Bible puts it: in the midst of life etc. etc.

I think about death a lot now. I should, I've seen it often enough. Once, a long time ago I refused to acknowledge it. I was young then and thought that I'd live for ever like all young men do.

Then, when I realised that I wouldn't, I was in fear of death. It hovered over me like a scourge. But now, with so many I've loved gone on that journey before me, it no longer frightens me. In fact, in a strange, perverse way I almost welcome it. It's the last unknown. The only taboo subject we seem to have left in a world I've seen change so fast as we head for the new century. The only subject that people don't talk about. We're in this life for such a short, precious time, but we don't treat our time as precious. We squander it on meaningless things and I'm so tired of wasting time. So that when death finally comes to me I want to embrace it. Love it like I've never managed to love anything or anyone properly in my time here in the land of the living.

Suddenly outside a car door slammed as loud as a pistol shot and I almost ducked. Melanie woke up. 'What are you doing?' she asked in a voice thick with sleep.

'Thinking,' I replied.

'What about?'

'Nothing much.'

'Come back to bed.'

'In a minute,' I said, and she rolled over and was asleep again almost immediately.

But I carried on talking as if she could hear me. 'I have dreams of leaving, you know, Mel,' I said softly. 'Dreams of a better place, but I doubt now if I'll ever find it. Sometimes I wonder if a better place even exists for someone like me.'

I knew what she'd say if she could hear me. 'Then go and find it.' But it's not that easy.

I turned back and looked into the glass again and watched myself watching myself. I didn't like what I saw. A middle-aged man who'd never fulfilled his promise or ambitions and now never would. A man who'd made so many mistakes that all the regrets and apologies that could be made would never wipe the slate clean. I pulled a clown's face at myself and knew that self-pity was the lowest of the emotions, but sometimes the only one that fitted the moment, especially on a rainy autumn night with the leaves falling outside and swirling down the gutters in the streets like the dreams of lost youth.

I lit another cigarette, went into the kitchen and found some juice in the refrigerator and filled a glass. I drank the juice standing by the stove then turned off the light and crawled back into bed and tried to warm the cold knot inside my belly with the night-time heat of Melanie's body, but it was still there when I finally fell asleep as a distant clock chimed two.

Twenty-four

WEDNESDAY MORNING, AFTER Melanie had gone to work I stood under the shower for a long time to ease the ache in my shoulders and legs. 'You're getting much too old for this lark,' I remarked to my reflection afterwards in the mirror as I shaved. But at least in the light of a new day I didn't feel as desperate as I had in the small hours when the spirits are always low, and the face I saw didn't repulse me quite as much, even with the lovely black eye that was maturing fast, so that was something. I grinned a wry grin through the shaving foam and wondered what to do next.

My mind was made up for me when the telephone rang as I was chewing on a slice of toast and raspberry jam twenty minutes later, still trying to finish the previous day's *Telegraph* crossword.

I dropped the paper, still doubtful about fifteen down, swallowed some tea to clear my mouth and picked up the receiver. 'Sharman,' I said.

'Is that the detective?' a male voice asked tentatively.

For one second I thought it might be Paul Jeffries and all my troubles about finding him and Meena were over. 'Yes,' I replied.

'Hello,' the voice said. 'My name's Henry. Henry Thorne.'

'You're Paul's friend?' I said, although his mother hadn't supplied a surname.

'That's right. I spoke to his mum last night. She said you wanted to talk to me.'

'I'm surprised you agreed.'

'She said you were all right. That you'd told that Paki fucker up the road to leave her alone.'

Khan's words in the restaurant came back to haunt me. Maybe we are all racist in this little country of ours. 'I wouldn't put it quite like that. I had a word. That's all.'

'Bloody good job. Then Peter phoned too. You know, Paul's brother.'

'I know,' I said.

'He warned me off talking to you. I never did take to him.

Bit of a bastard if you ask me.'

'I've met people I prefer,' I agreed.

'You're not alone there.'

'Well thanks for calling anyway,' I said.

'You ain't going to hurt him, are you?'

'Who – Paul or Peter?'

'Paul of course. Peter can look after himself.'

'With a little help from his friends,' I remarked. 'And then it can still go wrong.'

'What do you mean?'

'Long story.'

'I mean it. I won't talk if Paul gets into trouble.'

'He already is, if I'm any judge.'

'You know what I mean.'

'I know what you mean, and I'm not in the business of getting people into trouble, Henry,' I said soothingly. Although from my past record that wasn't strictly true. 'I try and get them out of trouble most of the time.'

'Right. I'll talk to you then. For what it's worth. Probably not much.'

'I'll be the judge of that.'

'OK.'

'When?' I asked.

'Today if you like. I ain't working. Got nothing else to do. You can buy me a drink.'

'It'll be a pleasure.' Although I somehow doubted that after the Paki crack. 'Where?'

'You know the Greyhound?' he asked.

'Streatham Common?'

'That's the one. The big bar in the front.'

'One o'clock suit you?'

'Fine. How will I know you?'

'I've seen your photograph,' I said. 'I'm a detective. I'll find you.'

Twenty-five

I GOT TO Streatham Common at ten to one. I parked the car on a side street a minute or two's distance away from the Greyhound and looked at myself in the rearview mirror after I'd switched off the engine. I was doing a lot of that lately – looking in mirrors. You do when you stop recognising yourself. These days I was seeing my grandad looking back at me. And sometimes, which was worse, my grandma. Yet in my youth I'd resembled neither of these dead relatives. I shrugged and ran my hand through my hair that was greying at the sides, shrugged again, left the car and walked to the pub.

It wasn't full and it wasn't empty and I stood inside the door and scoped the bar. I saw Henry after a moment and he saw me and raised an eyebrow. I think I would have recognised him from the photograph, but now his hair was much shorter, almost a crop, and instead of a suit he was wearing a pale blue Fred Perry shirt, a nylon windbreaker in a darker shade of blue, Levis with turn-ups and monkey boots. In front of him was a hardly touched pint, a pack of Superkings and a throwaway lighter.

I walked over to where he was sitting on a stool by the bar. 'Henry?' I said with a question mark.

He nodded.

'Nick Sharman.'

'Thought so.'

We shook hands. His palm was warm and wet.

'Drink?' I asked, surreptitiously wiping my hand on my thigh.

'Whisky chaser.'

I ordered a large Scotch for him and pint of lager for myself. The pub was warm, well lit and smelt of food from the hot plates on the far side of the bar. It was as easy being there as anywhere else on that chilly Wednesday lunchtime.

Whilst I waited to pay for our drinks I pulled up a stool and sat down next to him. Henry took a cigarette from the packet on the bar in front of him and offered me one. 'I'll stick to these,' I said and found my Silk Cut. But I took a light.

When my pint was in front of me and Henry's Scotch next to his pint, I said. 'So, have you heard from Paul recently?'

'Not for months.'

'Where was he?'

'Manchester. Working in a restaurant.'

'With Meena's brothers.'

He nodded.

'Did he tell you about her?'

'He was full of it. Told me he'd met the love of his life.'

'And?'

'And he didn't know what to do about it.'

'Did he tell you his options?'

'Sure. He was on the phone for ages.'

'And what were his options as far as he knew?'

'Easy. Forget all about her or for them to run away together.'

'And what was your advice?'

'I told him to get out. He was asking for trouble getting webbed up with a Paki girl.'

'Indian,' I corrected him.

'Whatever.'

'You don't like Asians. Is that it, Henry?' I enquired.

'Can take them or leave them as long as they don't interfere with me.'

'And you think Meena would've interfered with Paul.'

'Yeah I do as a matter of fact. Even if she was as beautiful as he said she was.'

I took the photo of Meena out of the envelope I was carrying in my pocket and showed it to him.

He pulled his mouth down. 'Tasty,' he said. 'I'll give you that. But Paul could never look after her proper. He's never had a steady job as long as I've known him. And you know what people think of mixed marriages.'

'Do they care much these days? Haven't times changed?'

'They care round here, I can tell you that. Shout out after them, call the kids all sorts.'

'So you told him to forget it.'

'Yeah.'

'No wonder he's not been in touch. Of course you know that he ignored your advice and left Manchester with her.'

'Sure I do. Stupid bastard.'

'And you haven't got any idea where they are?'

He shook his head.

'So what's the point of our meeting, Henry?' I said. 'Got no one to talk to? No one to buy you a drink?' I didn't want to antagonise him, but I was close. In fact the more I thought about it, the less I cared if I *did* antagonise him. He was no good to me. And not much use to himself as far as I could see.

'You've got black mates ain'tcha?' he said.

'I have had.'

'They're not real though, are they? Even their own kind call 'em coconuts. Black on the outside, white inside.'

I shrugged. 'So what?' I said.

'So nothing. I've seen 'em. Black mates and white mates having a right good time. But it ain't real.'

I decided to change the subject before Henry annoyed me more and I shoved his whisky glass up his nose. My body still ached and I wasn't in the mood.

'So would you help Paul if he came to you?'

'Course I bloody would. He's a mate.'

'Even though you disagree with what he's done.'

'I told you. He's a mate.'

Maybe he did know something and he was just a bit slow at getting round to it. 'That's good, Henry,' I said. 'I like that. A man who's loyal to his friends. And his mother?'

'What about her?'

'You'd help her too.'

'Sure. She's one of the best. A diamond.'

'But she's not asked.'

'No.'

'How about his brother Peter?'

'I told you, I don't like the geezer.' He looked at my black eye and smirked. 'Met him, have you?'

'A passing acquaintance.'

'He done that?'

I nodded.

'Looks like you didn't get on.'

'You could put it like that.'

'A ruck?'

'We had words.'

'You come out best?'

'More by luck than judgement. How do you know?'

'If you hadn't you wouldn't be walking today. Watch out. He bears a grudge.'

'I'll remember that. Now getting back to Paul. You know why I'm interested?'

'Her old man's hired you to find them.'

'Correct.'

'Yeah. Mum told me.'

'Mum?'

'That's what I call Mrs J. Always have done. My mum died.'

'Sorry.'

'Don't be. I was just a nipper.'

'I'm not out to harm Paul.'

'That's what Mum said.'

'So if you do hear…' I left the rest unsaid, then added, 'It might be worth your while.'

'Well I could certainly use the cash. The dole don't go far these days.'

'What do you do?' Not that I was interested.

'Anything. But there's too much cheap labour about…'

I cut him off before he started to tell me why. I knew where he was coming from. 'So bear it in mind,' I said. 'A bit of dough can't hurt. You've got my number.'

He nodded and looked morosely into his glass. 'Another drink?' he asked.

'No thanks,' I replied. 'I've got work to do.'

'Wish I had,' he said. 'And I meant another drink for me, not you.'

I called for a pint and another whisky for him. 'You'll find something,' I said as I waited to pay.

'Fat chance.'

'Well I've got to go,' I said. 'Ring me if anything turns up.'

'I'll do that,' he said, and I emptied my glass, slid off my stool and went back to the car.

Twenty-six

WHEN I GOT back home I called Khan at his business number. He answered himself. Democratic guy. No office version of Jyoti to run interference. Or maybe she was in the loo. 'Sharman,' I said.

'Ah Mr Sharman. How are things progressing?'

'I've got a mouse under my eye if that's any use to you,' I replied.

'A mouse?' he queried.

'I had a run in with Paul Jeffries' brother. He brought a couple of friends to the party.'

'What was the upshot?'

'Like I said, I got a black eye, but they came off second best.'

'I'm delighted. It shows that my faith in you was justified.'

'I was lucky. Apart from that, nothing. I need to come to Manchester. See a few people like we discussed. I've run out of people to talk to down here.'

'When?'

'Tomorrow would be good.'

'Very well. I'll organise a hotel. A double room, wasn't it?'

'That's right. I expect to arrive in the afternoon. Then we can meet for that dinner you promised. Meanwhile if you could smooth the way for me to speak to Meena's friends.'

'I've told you, I've already spoken to them, and they know nothing.'

'It doesn't hurt to speak to them again. Maybe they'll find it easier to talk to a stranger. You know how it is.'

'Indeed I do.' He sounded resigned. 'Very well, Mr Sharman, if you insist. I'll do my best, but as I told you I don't think it will be easy.'

'I'm sure you'll manage, Mr Khan. With all your clout, what could be easier?'

'I'm glad you have faith in me, Mr Sharman.' He was icily polite.

'Just as you have in me, Mr Khan. I'll leave the details in your capable hands then.'

'I'll get back to you within the hour with the reservation details.'

'I'll be at home.'

'Good. We'll meet tomorrow then.'

We made our farewells and hung up. Next I called Melanie at work. 'I'm off to Manchester tomorrow until the weekend. Still want to come?'

'Sure.'

'Can you get the time off?'

'Just watch me.'

'Fine.'

She hesitated for a moment.

'What?' I said.

'I was just wondering if I had enough clothes at your place for the trip.'

'You've got enough clothes at my place for a fortnight in the West Indies,' I said.

'Is that a problem?'

'No.'

'Good. I'll take your word for it. Have you got a bag I can borrow?'

'You use mine. I'll just stick a few things on top.'

'Nick, you're great.'

'And don't you forget it. Khan's organising a hotel. I'll check the train times.'

'And I don't have to do a thing.'

'Just be here.'

'Count on it.'

She arrived at six as full of excitement as a five-year-old going to the seaside. 'It's only grungy old Manchester,' I said.

'We've never been on holiday together before,' she said as she started tossing clothes into my old leather holdall.

'Who said this was going to be a holiday? And leave a bit of room for my stuff,' I protested.

'Don't be such a killjoy. There's some plastic bags under the sink for when this is full.'

'And guess whose clean shirts will go in them?' I said.

'Oh Nick, get a grip,' she said. 'It's going to be fun. Have you booked our tickets?'

'Of course.'

'And where are we staying?'

Khan had rung back with the details and I read them off the piece of paper I'd jotted them down on. Of course she was none the wiser, as was I.

'Sounds all right,' she said.

'Four star. Nothing but the best for the visiting detective and his trusty assistant.'

'You're great, Nick,' she said again, giving me a big hug. 'Now what are we going to eat?'

Twenty-seven

WE CAUGHT THE twelve-ten to Manchester on first class tickets with a lunch reservation. Not bad. At least Melanie was impressed even if I wasn't.

'The food's probably crap,' I said as we settled down. Me with the *Telegraph* crossword and *Mojo*, and her with *OK!* and *Hello!* magazines.

'It'll be great,' she said as the train slowly pulled out of Euston into the inner city hell where passengers can look through other people's windows and thank God they don't live like that.

'If you say so,' I remarked, and settled down with eight pages on Jimi Hendrix and she checked out Phil Collins' new gaff in Switzerland.

We went to eat at one, after I knew all I wanted to know about touring America in the 1960s, and she was *au fait* with the singing drummer and his new, young girlfriend's choice of wallpaper.

As it goes the lunch wasn't bad. Soup of the day was leek and potato, followed by lamb cutlets in a port sauce with *dauphinoise* potatoes and finishing with apple crumble and custard. Melanie passed on the crumble and had fruit sorbet.

'My tummy's getting too big,' she said by way of explanation.

'Looks all right to me,' I said, which is always the right thing to say to women, I've found in my little life.

'I've finally come on,' she confided.

'It's arrived at last,' I said.

'Don't sound so relieved. Don't worry, I'm not pregnant.'

'I never thought you were.'

'There was a bit of a haunted look there for a minute though.'

'Not on your life,' I said.

We lingered over coffee and brandy and had only just got back to our seats when we got into Manchester Piccadilly station.

It was raining by then. Big surprise.

We caught a cab at the station to the hotel that Khan had

booked for us. It wasn't a long journey but I saw from the taxi window that Manchester had changed since my last visit. The architecture was new and modern, not like I remembered. The city was trying for the new century, but then Manchester was always trying for something and failing. The hotel was located in an old insurance building where the foyer was massive and the rooms were small. But the bed was big enough, there was a whirlpool bath and a minibar which I raided for one of the half-bottles of champagne that nestled there. There were a lot of old photographs of the place as it had been, framed and screwed to the wall, presumably to deter insurance buffs. The foyer was where the bulk of the business had been done, hence the size, and I imagined the rooms were where the burghers of Manchester had plotted and planned.

'You'll have me drunk,' said Melanie as we toasted each other with the bubbly whilst Sky News buzzed on the TV in the background.

'That's the idea,' I replied.

'Don't forget I've got my period,' she said as she evaded my wandering hands.

'That doesn't stop us having a cuddle, does it?' I said.

'Business before pleasure. Hadn't you better call your client?'

'S'pose so,' I said and rang his office.

This time a woman answered and put me through when I identified myself. 'We're here,' I said.

'Did you have a good journey?' Khan asked.

'It was fine.'

'Is your accommodation satisfactory?'

'Can't complain.'

'Good. Now what I suggest is that we meet later for dinner at one of my restaurants. I'll have one of my men collect you at seven if that is to your liking.'

'Sounds all right to me,' I said. 'Seven it is.'

'Very well. We'll discuss your itinerary then. Meanwhile I hope that you'll enjoy your first day in Manchester.'

'I'll do just that,' I replied, put down the phone and reached for Melanie.

This time she didn't try to evade me.

Twenty-eight

So it was that we found ourselves, washed, dressed and with hair neatly combed, in the massive foyer of the hotel listening to a pianist playing Barry Manilow's greatest hits as the clock struck seven on a nearby tower and our driver arrived.

I had been expecting one of Khan's large, silent friends who'd been with him in London, but this bloke made them look like midgets. Although the foyer was huge he fitted it perfectly, almost filling the double doors as he came in and standing at least six foot five in his shiny suit, which was stretched almost to splitting point by his massive shoulders and arms, and he was wearing a turban in the colours of Manchester United Football Club.

'Could be our mentor and guide,' I said to Melanie as he entered and scoped the room.

'Or else he's got the biggest minicab in town.'

'Biggest something that's for sure,' I said.

'Don't be dirty.'

He spotted us and cocked his massive head and I knew it was us he'd been looking for.

'Looks like it's going to be a fun evening,' I said as I rose to greet him.

'Sharman?' he said when I looked up into his face. It was a long look, like The Statue of Liberty from the Staten Island ferry.

'Correct,' I replied.

'Rajah,' he said.

'Melanie,' I said by way of introduction to my companion. 'Meet Mr Rajah.'

'Just Rajah,' he said.

'Pleased to meet you, Rajah,' she said.

He grunted. 'Car's outside.'

'Then let's party on down.' That was me.

A black Mercedes with tinted windows was parked on double yellows outside the hotel and Rajah pulled open the back door for us. 'Cheers,' I said.

Another grunt was all I got in reply.

'Chatty,' I remarked to Melanie as we slid across the mustard-coloured leather upholstery in the back of the car.

'That's all right. I hate cabbies with too much to say,' she said.

'Maybe you'd better not let him hear you call him a cabbie,' I warned.

'I'll remember that, Nick.'

Rajah got into the driver's seat, started the car and pulled swiftly into the traffic. As he went he pushed a CD into the jaws of the player and if I was expecting more Ravi Shankar I was going to be bitterly disappointed. Instead, after a second I recognised a tune from the seventies. *Some Girls,* by Racey. A glam rock anthem. I pulled a face at Melanie. She pulled one back. When it finished it was followed by *Ballroom Blitz* by the Sweet.

I leant forward and said, 'You get off on this music, Rajah?'

He glanced round. 'Yes I do. I used to bodyguard The Glitter Band,' he said. 'Any objections?'

'Not me,' I replied. 'This is just fine.' Then to Melanie, 'Funny old world.'

Twenty-nine

IT WAS GETTING dark by then and the lights of Manchester were bright in the twilight. 'Not much like *Coronation Street*, is it?' said Melanie as we drove.

'I don't think anything is,' I remarked as the Sweet finished and *Mr Soft* by Steve Harley came on the speakers.

'A glitter fest,' I said under my breath. I didn't want to upset Rajah. I had a feeling he could cave in my chest with one fist. In fact I knew he could, and I'd had all the knocks I wanted for the time being.

It was only a short drive to where we were going, maybe fifteen minutes but by the time we got to our destination we'd had a quick lesson in what was hot on the charts between 1972 and the end of the decade.

Rajah pulled the car to the kerb outside a restaurant called the Eastern Promise, killed the engine, pushed open his door, eased himself out of his seat and opened the back door for us. Very polite. Mr Khan obviously instilled the right attitude in his employees.

I got out and helped Melanie on to the pavement and Rajah said, 'Mr Khan is inside.'

'Thank you,' Melanie and I chorused and we pushed through the door of the restaurant into the warm smell of herbs and spices and the embrace of a young Asian in a deep purple tuxedo, lilac shirt and pink bow tie. 'Lady and gentleman,' he trilled. 'What is your pleasure?'

I didn't elaborate. Instead said, 'I believe Mr Khan is expecting us. My name is Nick Sharman.'

'Mr Sharman and lady,' he carolled. 'Of course, Mr Khan is waiting.' He clapped his hands with joy and bowed us through to a large table at the back next to an aquarium full of fish with faces as long as Tory politicians on the last election night. Khan was sitting alone, and rose when he saw us arrive.

The manager pulled out chairs, got us all seated and popped napkins on our laps before he said, 'Something to drink, sir, madam. Mr Khan sir?'

'A beer,' I said, Melanie nodded agreement, Khan shook his head, and the manager walked fluidly towards the bar.

'Good evening,' said Khan. 'Forgive Ronit. He gets carried away when the boss is in.'

'He knows which side his nan bread is buttered then,' I said.

'What a shame you don't, Mr Sharman,' said Khan. 'But then I'm getting used to that.'

'Not at all,' I said. 'I'm beginning to enjoy this job more and more as every day passes. Even getting beaten up is a pleasure when I'm in your employ, Mr Khan.'

Khan sucked air through his teeth. 'I never know when you're joking, Mr Sharman. And I don't believe I've ever been introduced to your… assistant is it?'

'Sorry,' I said. 'Melanie Wiltse this is Mr Rajesh Khan. My principal and employer and the kind benefactor of our trip to Manchester. And Mr Khan, I think I may have exaggerated the assistant part.'

'I saw you at Ravi's restaurant in Streatham, Miss Wiltse,' said Khan as our beers arrived. 'And I cannot blame Mr Sharman for mixing business with pleasure.'

'Melanie please,' said Melanie, colouring slightly.

'And she *will* be taking notes,' I explained. 'She knows why we're here, in fact she convinced me to take the job. And of course anything you say to either of us is confidential.'

'Of course,' said Khan. 'So I'm indebted to you, Melanie. And I'm truly sorry about what happened to your face, Mr Sharman. I had no idea that violence would be involved when I offered you this job.'

'If there was no violence involved Nick wouldn't think he was earning his money,' said Melanie.

'She paints a rather lurid picture of my methods,' I said.

Melanie just gave me one of *those* looks in reply.

'Well I hope there will be no repeat of the incident,' said Khan. 'Now will you both choose from the menu before we get down to business.'

So we did.

Thirty

IT WAS A high class establishment as Indians go, at least by south London standards, which are the ones I'm used to, which meant that things like lamb cutlets, duck and trout were on the menu, and the portions were tiny, at inflated prices and tarted up with greenery and carrots cut into the shape of rosebuds. You know the deal.

'We get a lot of actors in here,' said Khan proudly when our dishes were delivered. 'The Granada studios are not far.'

'See what I mean,' I said to Melanie. 'Real life's not like *Coronation Street* at all.'

Khan looked puzzled but left it, and when our plates were full and our glasses charged with an expensive white wine, he said to me, 'I've made arrangements for you to see Meena's closest friends.'

I looked at him with interest over a forkful of okra.

'There are three of them. Dalgit and Geeta you can see tomorrow, Meena's English friend Caroline on Saturday, although I think you'll be wasting your time.'

'I've plenty of it,' I said.

'Yes I know, and I'm paying you well for it.'

'And I hope I earn it. Give me their names and addresses and I'll get started first thing.'

'No. No addresses. We have to do this my way. It's delicate, you see. It took me a lot of persuading for you to be allowed to see the Asian girls. The English girl wasn't easy either. So I've arranged for Rajah to ferry you back and forth, and he will stay with you during your interviews. With a family member present of course. People know Rajah, and trust him. He is one of my foremost lieutenants and he was very fond of Meena. He's known her since she was a child.'

'That's going to make it difficult to get them to be forth-coming,' I said. 'With half of Manchester sitting in.'

'These are young women, Mr Sharman,' said Khan. 'The Asian girls have led sheltered lives. As for Caroline, she is still at school and it took all my persuasive powers to get you an interview. Believe me you do it this way or not at all. And you will be alone. I'm sorry Melanie but that's how I arranged it.'

She nodded assent.

'Very well, Mr Khan,' I said. 'Have it your way. But it's not going to make my job any easier.'

'You wanted to meet these children,' said Khan. 'I was against it from the beginning. I don't like my family business being discussed by all and sundry.'

'But you want Meena back.'

'Of course. That goes without saying.'

I knew I was getting nowhere, and at least I could get to talk to Meena's friends even if I had to be heavily chaperoned to do it, so I changed the subject. 'These three are all girls,' I remarked. 'No boys.'

'Meena was not allowed to mix with boys.'

'She mixed with Paul Jeffries.'

'I've explained the circumstances of that.'

'Maybe that was why she ran away with him. Perhaps you should've been more liberal.'

'Liberation has nothing to do with it. Meena was promised to another.'

I was amazed that Melanie wasn't putting in her two penn'oth. Then of course she did. 'Isn't that rather an old-fashioned outlook, Mr Khan?' she said.

He focused his gaze on her. 'Fashion has nothing to do with it either,' he said. 'There is too much talk of fashion these days. I believe in the old ways. My marriage was arranged over fifty years ago when I was just a boy and my wife wasn't even born. She stayed chaste until our wedding night. We only met that very day, but we had over twenty good years together, so don't talk to me of fashion and liberation. I see the results of those things every day in my city. I see broken homes and delinquent children. I see drug addiction and the morality of alley cats. I see beggars on the streets and naked women in daily newspapers. Fashion. You have a daughter, Mr Sharman. I hope you never lose her because of fashion and liberal ways. Then you'll know what I'm talking about.'

There wasn't much either Melanie or I could add to that impassioned speech, and you never know, maybe he was right. In fact I almost *had* lost Judith to those very things, so we stayed silent and finished our meals in a rather subdued way.

Whilst the Irish coffees were being served to me and Melanie and I'd accepted a cigar from the box proffered by Ronit and she'd declined the same, Khan said, 'I've arranged for you to meet my sons also.'

'Good,' I replied. 'I've been looking forward to that. Where and when?'

'On Saturday evening we will gather for dinner.'

'Life's just one long feast when you're about, Mr Khan,' I said.

He half bowed in his seat. 'I do my best.'

I looked round the restaurant. 'And your best is very good,' I remarked. 'How many restaurants do you have?'

He flicked his fingers as if it were of no consequence. 'A dozen. Maybe more.'

'Not quite sure eh?' I said. 'I suppose it must be easy to lose track. Forget you've got a restaurant and then be pleasantly surprised when it's featured in the *Michelin* guide.'

He smiled. 'Your sense of humour gets stranger with the wine, Mr Sharman,' he said.

'You should see him when he gets on the brandy,' said Melanie. 'He's a laugh a minute.'

'You two seem well suited,' said Khan.

Crazy as bed bugs I think is what he meant but was too polite to say.

'We're just a pair of comedians,' I said. 'Two little rays of sunshine.'

'Perhaps you should get married,' he said, and smiled as I choked on the Cuban.

'I don't think so,' said Melanie. 'I don't think Nick is ready to settle down yet.'

'Don't leave it too long,' said Khan. 'Life is very short.'

And on that happy note we finished the meal.

Thirty-one

WHEN THE THREE of us left the restaurant, a man and woman were just coming in and I stepped politely aside to let them through the door. Outside Melanie grabbed my arm. 'Isn't she in *Coronation Street*?' she asked. 'The one they put in prison in the show.'

Khan looked back through the door. 'That's right.'

'See,' said Melanie triumphantly to me. 'It is like *Coronation Street* up here.'

'I didn't know they'd let her out,' I remarked.

'Don't be silly, it's not real,' said Melanie.

'What *is*?' I asked as she crossed the pavement, but no one was listening.

Rajah was standing by the kerb with the Mercedes, and there was a BMW 7-Series with a driver for Khan. 'Let me know how you get on with the girls,' he said as he shook our hands before climbing into the back of his car. 'It's been a pleasure, Melanie, Mr Sharman,' he added through the open window, but I don't think he really meant it. At least about me. Melanie was a different matter.

'A pleasure,' I said to Melanie as Rajah opened the back door of the Merc for us. 'I don't think so.'

'I'm beginning to wish I'd not kept on at you to take this job,' she said as she settled into the deep upholstery. 'You're right about him. He gives me the creeps.'

'Too late now. The money's almost spent. I was a bit behind on the mortgage.'

'Trust you.'

We got back to the hotel in a subdued mood and Rajah said, 'I'll pick you up tomorrow at ten,' to me as he deposited us outside.

'I can't wait,' I said.

We went upstairs to our room and Melanie made coffee and we sat on the bed and I said, 'This is a bust. They're not going to tell me anything. I don't know if Khan even wants Meena back. He's not making it easy.'

'What do you think he's spending all this money for then?' she asked.

'Fuck knows. Anyway let's go to bed and worry about it later.'

We did, but we weren't in the mood for fooling around, and we just lay together side by side and watched the car headlights from outside make patterns on the ceiling through the gap in the curtains until eventually we both fell asleep.

I'd ordered an eight o'clock call and we were up and finishing breakfast when Rajah arrived to collect me. The restaurant was at one end of the foyer so I spotted him as he asked for us at the desk and was pointed in our direction. 'He's here,' I said. 'What are you going to do today?'

'Shopping. I've heard there's some good places in town.'

'I'm sure there are. I bet all the actresses from *Coronation Street* shop at them too.'

'I wish I'd never mentioned that show,' she said as Rajah arrived at the table.

'Ready?' he grunted.

'As I ever will be. What time do you expect to get back here?'

'Mid-afternoon,' he said.

'I'll see you in the bar then,' said Melanie.

'Shop till you drop, babe,' I said and followed Rajah out into the drizzle to where the Mercedes was illegally parked again.

Thirty-two

WE DROVE THROUGH thickening rain into the suburbs of Manchester, which were very much like the suburbs of London as far as I could tell. Leafy and affluent, with Jeep Cherokees, Audis, BMWs and Jaguars parked in the streets and drives. All the way Gary Glitter's greatest hits were on the stereo. 'You really like this stuff, don't you?' I said to Rajah who had been silent throughout the entire journey.

'The Leader,' he said.

'But fallen on hard times.'

'He'll be back.'

'Did you miss him while he was away?' I asked.

'Yes.'

'Did you keep his picture up on your wall?'

Rajah looked over through slitted eyes. 'Funny,' was all he said.

I thought so. I was tempted to ask if he told those naughty boys not to call, but I thought he might take more offence.

Eventually we turned into a wide boulevard with detached houses separated by trees and shrubs on both sides of the road, and Rajah slid the Mercedes to a halt outside an imposing set of iron gates. 'First one,' he said. 'Her name's Dalgit. They were at school together. They've known each other since childhood.'

''K,' I said, and went to open the door. He put a meaty hand on my arm. 'Why are you doing this?' he asked as the rain spattered the windscreen in front of me.

'What?'

'Looking for Meena and that boy.'

'Because it's my job. I'm a detective and I'm being well paid.'

'Meena was my friend. I've known her since she was born. She is a beauty.'

I didn't know quite where we were heading with this. 'I know,' I said. 'I've seen the photo.'

'The photo doesn't do her justice.'

'I'm sure it doesn't.'

He said nothing.

'And?' I asked.

'And I don't want to see her hurt.'

'Nor do I.'

'Is that right?'

'Yes. I just want to see her back safe.'

'But how safe would she be?'

I shrugged his hand off and said, 'What's all this about? I thought you would want what Khan wants.'

'I do up to a point.'

I felt we were getting on to dangerous ground. 'Is there something I don't know?'

He grinned, showing large white teeth. 'There's lots you don't know.'

'Like what?'

'You'll find out.'

'Something tells me that almost everyone has a hidden agenda up here.'

'Maybe, maybe not.'

'You're not being very clear.'

He shrugged.

'And something else tells me that Mr Khan wouldn't be happy if I told him about this conversation.'

'I'd deny it ever took place, then I'd find you and you might end up in the canal swimming with the fishes.'

Shit. I believed he was serious.

'Rajah,' I said. 'I *don't* know what's going on here, honest. I'm just trying to earn a crust. But if there *is* something I should know just tell me. It won't go any further, Scout's honour.'

He looked at me hard and long and sucked his teeth. 'We'll see,' he said. 'Just be careful.'

Believe me I was going to be.

Thirty-three

H E OBVIOUSLY WASN'T going to elaborate, so I opened the door and ducked through the rain close on Rajah's heels, up to the porch of the house and he rang the doorbell.

It was answered by a tall, middle-aged Indian gentleman with a beard shot through with grey, wearing a charcoal suit, white shirt and plain tie. 'Rajah,' he said.

'Mr Singh,' Rajah replied and they embraced.

'Any news on Meena?' asked Mr Singh.

'No. This is Mr Sharman, the gentleman Mr Khan told you about.'

Singh surveyed me and stood back to allow us to enter. Once inside he shook my hand, but it was barely a touch. 'I don't like doing this to Dalgit. She's distressed enough already about Meena. I'm sure this will just be a waste of time.'

'I understand,' I reassured him. 'I have a daughter of my own in her teens. Believe me, I'll keep it short and simple.'

'She's in the lounge,' he said and pointed to an open door beside an imposing staircase. The house was silent and chilly and extremely neat.

I went into the room where a slight, pretty girl in a sari was standing by the mantelpiece of a dead fire. 'Dalgit, this is Mr Sharman,' said Mr Singh. 'He has a few questions for you. You know Rajah of course. Please let us all be seated. Does anyone require refreshments?'

I shook my head and Rajah did the same, and all four of us took our seats. Me on a straight-backed chair next to a small table, Rajah and Mr Singh on a long sofa and Dalgit on a matching armchair. I moved my chair to be in front of her. 'Dalgit,' I said. 'I know this is upsetting, but Meena's father has asked me to find her. You were her friend. Maybe you know something…'

She went to deny it and I smiled.

'… I know. You've thought long and hard, but this is my job, and you may know something important that you haven't even thought of. When did you last see her?'

'A few days before she left. We went to the cinema.'

'What did you see?'

'*Titanic*. For about the sixth time.'

'You obviously like the film.'

'It's wonderful. Leonardo DiCaprio is *so* dishy.'

Mr Singh made a sound of dissent but I ignored him. 'My daughter likes him too,' I said. 'Did Meena tell you she was leaving?'

'No.'

'No indication at all.'

She shook her head.

'Did you know she was seeing Paul Jeffries?'

She looked at her father, then shook her head. 'Only as a friend. In the group.'

'But you had no idea it was serious?' I pressed.

'No.'

'And have you heard from her since?'

Another shake of the head.

'You'd tell me if you had?'

She looked me straight in the eye and said, 'Yes. I miss Meena. I wish she was here. We used to have fun.'

Something told me that fun was in short supply in this household. I smiled. 'Of course you would. Do you think any of her other friends have?'

'I don't know. I don't think so. Geeta would've told me, I'm sure.'

'How about Caroline?'

'We don't see each other.'

'Fair enough. That's it, Dalgit. Thanks for your help.'

'I haven't. Helped you, that is.'

'Yes you have.' I took one of my cards from my pocket and put it on the arm of her chair. 'If you think of anything or hear from Meena please get in touch with me. With your father's permission of course.'

I looked at Mr Singh and he nodded. He seemed pleased the interview was over. I stood up. 'Thank you both,' I said. 'We'll be off now.'

Rajah rose and Mr Singh showed us to the door. 'I told you it would be a waste of time,' he said as he opened it.

'Don't worry,' I said. 'Most of my time is.'

Thirty-four

RAJAH AND I ate lunch in a balti house in another suburb. But an inner one this time that was more like I'd remembered Manchester as being. It was full of high rises and the restaurant itself was in a row of mean shopfronts, half of which were empty and boarded up, and there was a metal shutter over the window decorated with graffiti that was kept permanently pulled down as far as I could tell. Left to my own devices I would've been sure the place was derelict.

But the food was good, better in fact than the poncey place we'd eaten in on the previous evening. I had straight lamb balti with bread, and because the place wasn't licensed, a Coke. Rajah had chicken. The ambience was crap and the waiter picked wax out of his ear whilst he served us, but I enjoyed the meal.

Rajah opened up a bit about his life as we ate. He was an old rock and roller at heart and had toured with loads of top bands as a minder before he'd webbed up with Khan. He still missed life on the road. 'I could've worked with Oasis,' he said. 'I know their mum.'

'Maybe it was for the better you didn't,' I said picking a hair off my plate. 'You might not have got on with them.'

'They'd be in a lot less trouble if I was along,' he replied. 'I'd keep those boys in line.'

Looking at the great shoulders inside his distressed leather jacket I was sure he could.

The second interview of the day followed the lines of the first, except this time both Mum and Dad were in attendance. Geeta told me much the same as Dalgit. She didn't know about Meena and Paul except as friends. She didn't know where Meena was, hadn't heard from her since she left, and missed her badly. I believed the girl and didn't stay long, it seemed like just another waste of time. When we came out of the house, Rajah looked at me with an 'I told you so' face and I didn't argue. 'Back to the hotel,' I said and he concurred.

When I got back to the hotel Melanie was waiting in the bar

on a roll from a hard day's shopping in the boutiques of Manchester. 'Get anything good?' I asked.

'Plenty,' she replied. 'There's some sexy underwear shops in this town. I might try some of it on for you later.'

'I don't think I'm in the mood,' I said. 'I wouldn't appreciate it. Save it for when we get home. Anyway I didn't think you were into stiff things up your jacksie.'

'This is all pure silk.'

'It's tempting, but I still think it'd be wasted on me tonight.'

'What's the matter?' she asked as I sipped at an overpriced bottle of beer.

'I get the feeling I'm being pissed on from a great height,' I said. 'It occurs to me that some people don't want to me find Meena, and I don't know why.'

'Is your fee refundable?' she asked only half jokingly.

'Not if I've got anything to say about it. Let's get cleaned up and go out and eat. And not bloody Indian for a change.'

Thirty-five

THE RECEPTIONIST AT the desk downstairs in the foyer told us that the best Chinese restaurant in Manchester was just around the corner, and she phoned through and got us an immediate reservation. You wouldn't get that treatment in a London hotel. I thanked her with a fiver, she gave us the directions and we decided to walk.

It took about ten minutes through the back streets behind the hotel, and when we arrived the *maître d'* showed us to a table by the window and we ordered gin and tonics. 'So what's the problem?' Melanie asked me when they arrived.

'Rajah's got some hidden agenda,' I said after I told her about the interviews I'd had with the two Asian girls.

'What? I thought he was Khan's number one.'

'He may well be, but I'm sure he knows more than he's telling.'

'You think he knows where Meena is?'

'I don't know. But somebody in this town does.'

'What about the girl you're seeing tomorrow?'

'Dunno. She's English. Maybe she'll know more and be willing to tell me. But with Rajah and members of the immediate family in attendance, who knows. This whole trip has been a waste of time so far.'

'But a nice little holiday.'

'You didn't have to sit in the car with Rajah for half the day listening to T. Rex and Gary Glitter.'

'I'm sure it wasn't that bad.'

'Not really. It took me back a bit I must admit.'

'To when you wore tartan trousers and a satin jacket?'

'Don't remind me. We haven't had the Rollers on yet. But I expect we will.'

'It'll be something to look forward to.'

The waiter appeared and we ordered one of the recommended meals for two. I couldn't be bothered to choose anything. I was feeling pissed off and a bit annoyed that our trip to Manchester was becoming a walk up the garden path. I was determined to get to the bottom of the case and find Meena and Paul, and I knew that if I did it would be despite the so-called help I was getting rather than because of it.

But at least when the food arrived it was as good as its reputation, and after a couple of bottles of wine and a few brandies I was feeling better as we walked to the hotel through the back streets again.

Better, that was, until we turned into the road directly behind the hotel and I heard the roar of a car engine behind us, the screech of tyres as it took off at high speed, and when I looked back I was blinded by its headlights as it bounced up on the narrow pavement and headed straight for us.

'Shit!' I shouted, shoved Melanie in the direction of an alley off to the side of us, and leapt in the opposite direction myself to try and get as much distance between us as was possible. The car powered its way in our direction hitting the wall and throwing sparks from its bodywork as it zigzagged crazily towards us.

The car missed me by an inch and its slipstream tugged at my clothes as it passed me, crashed back off the pavement over the kerb and shot round the corner out of sight.

I didn't get the make or licence number. All I saw was that it was a dark, teardrop-shaped saloon, probably a Ford or a Vauxhall.

I stood shaking in the deserted street for a second then remembered Melanie. 'Mel,' I called. 'Are you OK?'

A bedraggled figure limped out of the alley. 'What happened?' she said tearfully as I went to her and held her tightly.

'Somebody tried to kill us. Or more likely me,' I said. 'Are you hurt?'

'No, not really. But someone should empty those dustbins. Christ knows what's in them.'

I held her at arm's length and looked at her in the faint light from a lamppost a few yards away. 'Yeah, you stink. Jesus. What did you fall into?'

'Thanks a lot. I don't like to think, ' she replied. 'But whatever it was it was past its sell-by.' And we both started to laugh hysterically with relief.

Thirty-six

THE SAME RECEPTIONIST was on duty when Melanie and I limped back into the hotel and her eyes widened with alarm at the state of the pair of us. See, I always limp a bit from an old injury, but Melanie had broken the heel off one of her shoes and laddered both legs of her dark tights so she showed long strips of white skin through them, which didn't help. And she was covered in garbage, some of which had adhered to me when we'd embraced, so we looked pretty bad I've got to admit. 'What happened to you?' the receptionist asked. 'Are you all right?'

'A bit of an accident,' I replied.

'Do you need an ambulance? A doctor?'

'All I need is the room key and a hot bath,' said Melanie rather crossly, and who could blame her, the state she was in. So much for a nice little holiday.

'Of course. Three-oh-seven, wasn't it?' said the girl.

'That's the one,' I replied.

She passed over the key and we ran the gauntlet of stares from the other residents *in situ* as we headed for the lift.

When we got to the room Melanie stripped to the buff whilst I ran a bath for her then got undressed myself. I put all our clothes into the laundry bag provided and forced it into the wastepaper basket. We weren't going to wear any of that stuff again. Then dressed in one of the courtesy bathrobes I joined her in the bathroom with a couple of large brandies.

'What the hell happened there?' she demanded through the steam as I handed her one of the drinks.

'Someone tried to warn us off, or worse,' I replied. 'That sort of thing happens from time to time. Remember Chris Grant and his pals?' I was referring to some villains I'd had dealings with in the case of a missing wife earlier that year. It was during my investigations that I'd met Melanie.

'How could I forget?' she asked.

'It's not all wine and roses, this job,' I said.

'I know that.'

'I'm just sorry you got involved.'

'Who do you think it was?' she asked. 'In the car, I mean.'

'Your guess is as good as mine at the moment,' I replied. 'But I intend to find out.'

Whilst she was drying herself off I ran a bath for myself and afterwards I lay with Melanie in my arms, as she tossed and turned and mumbled to herself as she slept.

Yes, I thought as I lay there listening to the early morning Manchester traffic outside. I'll find out all right.

Thirty-seven

THE NEXT MORNING Melanie was back to normal apart from some soup bowl sized bruises on her ribs and bottom. 'Snap,' I said when she showed them to me. 'I've got a set just like that myself.'

'Very funny.'

'Christ, we must've looked a state last night,' I said. 'Covered in muck, stinking to high heaven, and me with a face like the loser in a light-heavyweight contest that went the full fifteen rounds.'

'That poor girl behind reception,' she said, with the first smile of the day.

'I bet she was glad we were staying in her hotel,' I said. 'Just the sort of high-class clientele they need.'

'Do you think maybe she thought we'd done a runner at the Chinese restaurant and got caught?' said Melanie.

'Maybe. I doubt whether she'll recommend that place again in a hurry.' And we started to laugh so hard again that the tears were running down our faces by the time we'd finished.

After that the mood lightened. We took our bruised and battered bodies downstairs to the restaurant and were finishing breakfast when Rajah appeared as arranged.

'You take care of yourself today,' I said to Melanie as I got up to go.

'I'm not going anywhere.'

'That's good. We'll go back to London tomorrow, and I'll treat you to a new outfit to make up for the one that got ruined yesterday.'

'I can't wait.'

'Have fun then,' and I leant over and kissed her before joining Rajah by the door.

It was still drizzling a little as we set off and I said, 'Doesn't it ever stop raining in this town?'

'Not so's you'd notice,' he replied.

'Someone tried to kill us last night,' I said as we stopped at some lights.

Rajah looked over. 'Really,' he said.

'Really.'

'Not for the first time by the looks of it.' He glanced over and smiled as he looked at my face. He'd never referred to it before. And the expression on his face pissed me off.

'That was different,' I said as calmly as possible. 'At least they didn't wait for a dark night down a back alley.'

'Is that so? Down a back alley was it? People should be warned about back alleys. People don't get into trouble in back alleys when I'm about.'

'But you weren't about, were you?'

'Can't be everywhere at once.'

'That's true.'

'So tell me, what happened? Someone try to mug you for that flash watch of yours?'

'No. Someone aimed a car at us.'

'Dangerous places Manchester back alleys. Lots of drunks and junkies driving about. Could've been an accident.'

'I don't think so.'

'So what do you think?'

'I think someone's trying to warn me off.'

'And?'

'Bad decision. It makes me want to find Meena all the more. I'm funny like that. Especially when they involve my friends. I can look after myself but Melanie's a different matter. She's not involved. She's off limits. Putting her in the frame doesn't frighten me off, it just pisses me off. Got any ideas?'

'About what?'

'About where Meena is. About who's trying to put the frighteners on me.'

'No idea.'

'Fair enough. But like I say if you should hear a whisper, let it be known it's just made me all the more determined to finish the job.'

'I'll do that,' he said.

Thirty-eight

THE INTERVIEW WITH Caroline Lees, Meena's English friend, was different from the other two. The house she lived in was slightly smaller than the Asian houses we had visited the previous day, and semi-detached. There was an Audi convertible with the top up, on this year's plate parked in the drive.

Rajah and I walked up the garden path and he rang the bell. A stressed-out looking man answered after a moment, dressed in a denim shirt and cords. He was about my age but time had been less kind to his hair, which was retreating across his scalp at a rate of knots. 'Rajah,' he said.

'Good morning, Mr Lees,' said Rajah. 'This is Mr Sharman who's working for Mr Khan. Mr Sharman, Mr John Lees.'

'Nick,' I said with an outstretched hand and what I hoped was a friendly smile.

Lees didn't reciprocate. 'You'd better come in,' he said.

Inside it wasn't as neat and sterile as the Asian houses had been, and looked lived in and rather run down. Lees led us into the living room where the TV was showing a kids' Saturday morning show with the sound turned low, and Rajah and I sat down.

'I'll get Caroline,' said Lees. 'She's in her room. My wife's out at the shops with my son,' he explained rather unnecessarily I thought. He went to the foot of the stairs and shouted, 'Caroline. Come down please.'

There was no answer. 'She's probably got her headphones on. I won't be a moment,' and he vanished upstairs.

We heard raised voices and a minute or two later John Lees reappeared followed by a tall blonde girl in a charcoal sweater and a short black skirt over dark tights. I imagined under normal circumstances she was extremely pretty, but that morning her mood was such that her face just exuded a sullen aspect which did nothing for her features.

'This is my daughter Caroline,' he said. 'Rajah, you know, and this is Mr Sharman who's looking for Meena.'

Caroline Lees made no comment.

I stood at our introduction and held out my mitten. She ignored it. Like daughter, like father.

Good start.

'Hello Caroline,' I said. 'My name's Nick.'

If she could've looked less interested I'm sure she would, but I doubt if that would've been possible.

'Would you like to sit down?' I asked.

She shrugged, but took a straight-backed chair and stared at the TV screen as if nothing else in the world existed. John Lees noticed and snapped the set off with the remote. 'I was watching that,' she said.

'You can watch it later,' said John Lees.

'I want to watch it now.'

'Caroline,' he said exasperatedly.

'You were good friends with Meena, I believe,' I said to break the tension in the room.

She shrugged again. So far she hadn't spoken directly to me, but I was used to that from teenage girls with the hump at being disturbed on a Saturday morning. I've had it from Judith enough times.

'Have you heard from her since she went away?' I asked.

She looked at Rajah and her father and shook her head but I was sure she was lying.

'I'm only trying to help,' I said. 'Her family misses her.'

She spoke for the first time then. 'Is that right?' she asked.

'Yes,' I replied.

'And her family really love her, do they?'

'As far as I know.'

'Then you don't know much.'

I was more than willing to concede that. 'Like what?'

'Like they threatened to kill her and Paul.'

'Caroline,' said John Lees again, but I saw a spark of fear in his eyes as he spoke.

'Do you believe that?' I asked.

She nodded.

'So you have spoken to her.'

'Maybe.'

'Caroline,' John Lees interrupted. 'If you know anything please tell Mr Sharman.' But somehow I got the impression that was the last thing he wanted.

'I'm not going to hurt her,' I said.

'You won't have to, Sanjay and Deepak will do that for you.'

'In fact I won't let her be hurt.'

'And how are you going to stop them?'

'I'm sure it's not as bad as you think. You know what family arguments are like. Things are said in the heat of the moment.'

She laughed mirthlessly. 'Is that what you think? Not in that kind of family.'

'*Caroline*,' said John Lees for the third time.

'All right, Dad,' she said 'We know. Mr Khan puts the food on our table and the clothes on our backs. We mustn't say anything bad about him, must we?'

'He's not going to hurt Meena or her boyfriend,' he said.

'You don't know them. Not Sanjay and Deepak. They'll do anything to get her back.'

'But not murder, surely,' I said.

'Anything,' she repeated. 'So why don't you just leave me alone.'

'If you do speak to her,' I said leaning closer, 'tell her she can trust me. I won't let any harm befall her, I promise. I've got a daughter roughly the same age as you and Meena, Caroline, and she's the most precious thing in the world to me. I'd never let anyone hurt her and the same goes for Meena. All I want to do is to speak to her. After that it's her choice what she does.'

'Do you mean it?' said Caroline Lees in a small voice as if we were the only two people in the room.

'I promise.' I knew she knew something, but I also knew she wasn't going to divulge it with her father and Rajah there.

I took out another of my cards and wrote the name and phone number of the hotel on the back along with our room number. 'If you hear anything or Meena gets in touch you can reach me in London on either of the numbers on the front. Or she can. I'm in Manchester till tomorrow at this hotel. Maybe you'll remember something before I go.'

'I doubt it,' she said.

'Well, whatever,' I replied. 'I'll leave you alone now.' I stood up. 'Mr Lees, thank you for your time. Rajah, let's go.'

Caroline stood up and stalked out before us and upstairs to her room without a word of farewell.

John Lees shook his head. 'Sorry,' he said.

'Don't mention it,' I replied. 'Thanks again for your time.' And with that Rajah and I went back to the car.

'What do you think?' he asked.

'Dunno,' I replied. 'You know what it's like when you're their age.'

'I can't remember,' he said, started the car and headed it back into the direction of central Manchester.

Thirty-nine

MY MEETING WITH Khan and his sons didn't go much better. In fact it didn't go at all. It was at Deepak, the eldest's restaurant. I decided it was better if Melanie stayed back at the hotel. She moaned and groaned, but I reminded her of our narrow escape the previous evening. 'You stay here,' I said. 'Get room service. Watch TV. I won't be long and we'll be back in London tomorrow.'

'Thank God for that,' she said. 'I'm fed up with this place.'

'Me too. I've never felt so unwelcome for years.'

'You amaze me.'

'Funny.'

'And what about Paul and Meena?'

'I think I'm going to bow out. There's something smells bad here, and it isn't the chicken vindaloo.'

'Maybe it's best, Nick. I think I was wrong keeping on at you to take the case.'

'Now she tells me,' I said.

Rajah picked me up in the Merc at seven. The restaurant was located on what the locals call the Curry Mile. It was neither as large or as salubrious as the one where Melanie and I had met Khan. And there were no stars of the silver screen sampling the onion bhajis, or for that matter outgoing Asians in pastel outfits to greet us. This time Rajah parked the car and accompanied me inside. 'Hungry?' I asked.

He just shrugged.

The place was in semi-darkness and there was a CLOSED sign on the door. Rajah let us in with a set of keys and locked the door behind us. The place was empty, some tables set for meals and some not, but the usual sitar music was playing softly and I could smell food cooking. There was a table for six laid at the back of the restaurant where the single light came from and Rajah led me straight there. Khan and two young Asians were already *in situ*.

Khan introduced us. Deepak was heavily built with a beard and his brother Sanjay was slim and lithesome with a thin moustache like Clark Gable, but there the similarity ended.

Rajah and I joined the trio and a solitary waiter appeared from further back in the darkness. The whole deal was beginning to get to me. I felt I was being set up in some way, not for the first time since the whole affair started, and I didn't like it. After asking my preference Deepak called for beer for me and water for the rest.

'So have you had any success on your visit here, Mr Sharman?' he asked when the drinks had been served.

'Not much. I managed to escape being run down by a car last night and I asked a few people questions they weren't prepared to answer, that's all.'

'Is that where you got the black eye?' asked Sanjay.

'No. That was Paul Jeffries' brother. He thought I was trying to strong-arm his mother. Like you and your brother did.'

Sanjay gave me a dirty look with his dark brown eyes.

'What car?' interrupted Khan the elder.

'Didn't you tell your boss about my lucky escape?' I asked Rajah. 'That was a bit remiss of you. Someone tried to kill me and Melanie last night with the sharp end of a motor. They damn nearly succeeded too.'

'Why didn't you tell me about this?' demanded Khan of Rajah.

'A scally probably,' he replied offhandedly.

I wasn't going to argue. It was pointless. Instead I directed my attention back to Khan's sons.

'It's been suggested to me that you don't want Meena back at all,' I said.

'What do you mean?' demanded Deepak.

'I mean that I've heard that you only want her found so that you can kill her and Paul.'

Deepak exploded in a burst of laughter. 'Kill my own sister? What nonsense. Who told you that?'

'Paul's mother, for one. And Meena's friend Caroline Lees this morning. I'm sure Rajah's passed *that* nugget of information on.'

'Rubbish,' said Sanjay. 'Of course we want her back. Besides, who was going to kill them, may I enquire?'

I cocked my hand like a gun in Rajah's direction. 'How about this big fella here? Isn't that why he's been with me all the time? Normally I carry out my investigations alone.'

'Apart from your charming assistant of course,' said Khan. 'By the way, where is she tonight?'

'Back at the hotel,' I said. 'I felt it was safest after what happened last night. Accidents can come in pairs.'

'So what do you intend to do?' he asked.

'I intend to go back to London tomorrow, work out how much these last few days have cost you, deduct it from the money you gave me and return the rest. I want no part of this.'

'Chickening out?' asked Sanjay.

I was getting to dislike that boy intensely. If he didn't get out of my sight soon, or me out of his, I was going to have to attempt cosmetic surgery with my right hand. 'No,' I replied as gently as possible. 'But I'll have nothing to do with murder.'

'I've heard you've had a great deal to do with murder in the past,' said Khan.

'Been making enquiries?' I asked. 'Who imparted that bit of information, pray?'

'Some policemen friends of mine.'

'Nice friends you've got.'

'Useful.'

'But not at getting your daughter back.'

'They've been close.'

'But not close enough, obviously. Maybe you aren't paying them enough.'

'Sufficient.'

'Then I'll leave them and you to it.'

'Very well, Mr Sharman,' said Khan. 'Please yourself.'

'I will,' I said and got up from my seat.

'You're not leaving,' said Khan.

'You wanna bet?'

Then it got nasty. Both Deepak and Sanjay reached under their jackets and produced shiny 9mm pistols and in tandem pulled back the hammers with the nasty little oily clicks they make. 'Not without our father's permission,' said Deepak.

'You want to be careful,' I said with more bravado than I felt. 'Those things can go off.'

'So they can, Mr Sharman,' said Sanjay. 'And I think it's you that needs to be careful.'

Shit, I thought. So this is what it comes down to. Shot dead in a sleazy little northern curry house and probably ending up in the meat korma. To live and die in Manchester. I looked down and said to him, 'Do you really think I need *anyone's* permission to go when I want to?'

'In this case yes,' he replied.

'Then think again, buddy,' I said and turned on my heel and walked away from the table with muscular spasms running up and down my back.

'The door's locked,' Deepak said as I went.

'Stone walls do not a prison make nor iron bars a cage,' I said as I went, quoting *To Lucasta, Going Beyond the Seas* by Richard Lovelace 1618–1658. Strange what you pick up in a long and interesting life. On the way I picked up a chair. It had a wooden frame painted gold with a purple plush seat but it felt solid enough and it was. Solid enough to smash the glass out of the door and let me walk through, much to the amazement of a passing couple on the way to a night out. 'They didn't want me to go until I'd finished all my supper,' I said to them as I dropped the remains of the chair on to the pavement, but they said nothing in reply. No one from inside the restaurant said or did anything either.

Luckily I saw a Manchester taxi outside with its roof light on and hailed it. I was back at the hotel within twenty minutes and went straight to the room still shaking. The door was locked. I knocked and after a second Mel's voice said, 'Who is it?'

'It's me. Let me in.'

The door cracked and she said, 'Are you alone?'

'Absolutely. What's the matter?'

She pulled the door all the way and I went in. 'What is it?' I said.

She pointed and for the first time I noticed a figure sitting in the armchair by the little dining table.

It was Caroline Lees.

Forty

'WHAT'S SHE DOING here?' I said, rather brusquely, I've got to own up. But I was pissed off. It had been a lousy day, a rotten week, an unspeakable year and I was pretty fed up with the whole kit and caboodle of my life. Caroline Lees hadn't been exactly pleasant to me when I saw her on her ground that morning. Now she was on mine why should I be any different to her? Besides it's easier to beat up on a teenage girl and get away with it than it would've been to win a punch-up with the Khan clan and Rajah at the restaurant. I was still smarting from my little run in with them and I needed a target. I felt I'd let myself down walking out like I did. And I'd let down Meena and Paul.

At least I should've hit someone.

'She came looking for you and found me,' said Melanie. 'And don't be so horrible.'

'If this is about Meena you're too late,' I said to Caroline who looked much smaller here than in her house. She was wearing a little minidress with sheer dark tights and Doc Martens, and a dark blue coat was draped over the back of her chair. In front of her was a can of Diet Coke and a glass with a couple of cubes of ice melting in the bottom.

'Why?' she asked in a tiny voice. I swear she was frightened of me and that didn't make me feel any better.

'Because I just quit,' I explained in a softer voice. 'I finally met Meena's brothers and was not impressed.'

'Thank God,' said Caroline.

'How's that?' I asked.

'I lied today when I saw you.'

'Big surprise,' I replied. 'You and just about everybody else I've met lately.'

'Nick,' said Melanie harshly. 'Don't be so vile. Why don't you listen to what Caroline has to say.'

'Sorry,' I said wearily and I was. Sorry and weary and ready to go home and forget everything about the Khan case. I sat on the bed and washed my face with dry hands. My eyes felt like they were full of grit and all I wanted to do was to fall back on to the mattress and sleep for a week.

But I didn't. I blinked a couple of times and smiled at Caroline. 'OK,' I said. 'Tell me everything.'

Forty-one

CAROLINE POURED SOME more Coke into her glass and took a sip. 'I don't know where to start,' she said.

I sat forward on the bed, put my elbows on my knees and looked at her in what I hoped was a sympathetic and understanding way. 'At the beginning is best,' I said. 'Go on to the end, then stop. If I've got any questions I'll ask them then. Is that OK?'

She nodded meekly.

'Go on then,' I said.

'I knew about Meena and Paul from the beginning,' she explained. 'Meena couldn't talk to any of her Asian friends or relatives. They'd've told Mr Khan. But I was telling the truth about one thing this morning. They do want to kill Meena and Paul.'

I heard a sharp intake of breath from Melanie.

'I couldn't tell you anything in front of my dad and Rajah. Dad's terrified of Mr Khan. Frightened he'll lose his job. He'll never get another. Not as good anyway. That's why I came here. You knew, didn't you?'

I nodded. 'I knew you were hiding something.'

'That's why you told me you were staying here, isn't it?'

I smiled and nodded. 'Yes.'

'Did you think I'd get in touch?'

'I hoped you would.'

'I'm supposed to be at a party. That's how I got out tonight. I'll get into terrible trouble if Dad finds out.'

'Then we won't let him. Find out I mean,' I said. 'Carry on about Meena.'

'She didn't want it to happen with Paul,' she continued. 'She just wanted to be friends. But something happened and she fell in love with him. He's older and a bit rough, but he really cares for Meena. She was a virgin until…' She hesitated.

'Until what?' I said, fearing some further catastrophe.

'… Until they got married,' said Caroline quietly.

The words hung in the air like smoke. 'Jesus,' I said. 'Legally married?'

She nodded.

'That'll put the cat amongst the pigeons. Khan won't be pleased.'

'Meena's terrified,' said Caroline. 'Especially now she's pregnant.'

'Pregnant too,' I said, getting up, going to the minibar and freeing a beer from its chilly sentence inside. 'That's terrific.'

'I spoke to Meena tonight,' said Caroline. 'She knows all about you.'

'How?'

'From Paul's mother. They've spoken on the phone. You went to see her. She liked you. She said you told off the man in the corner shop. He was spying on her for Mr Khan. Now he won't look at her.'

'Well that's something,' I said. 'Mrs Jeffries told me lies too. She said she hadn't heard from them.'

'Did you really expect her to tell you?' said Caroline with an understanding that surprised me.

'No,' I replied. 'In fact I was surprised she let me through the door.'

'She said you had a kind face.'

'It's my fortune,' I replied. 'Maybe that's why I'm broke.'

Caroline laughed.

'So where are they?' I asked.

'I can't tell you. Not yet.'

'When?'

'When you promise to help Meena.'

'I don't know if I can make that promise. I was hired by her father.'

'And now you've left. You said that.'

'That's right.'

'And Melanie told me you hated this job. That you were more on Meena's side than Mr Khan's.'

'Thanks, Mel,' I said.

'So help Meena,' Caroline pressed.

'What can I do?'

'Get them somewhere safe so she can have her baby in peace.'

'I'm just one person,' I said. 'What about the police? The social services?'

'They've been to them…They're no good…Every time they

think they're safe Mr Khan finds out and they have to run away again…You don't know him…He's got people everywhere who owe him…' She suddenly seemed much older than her years. 'You don't understand how powerful he is… And her brothers…' She hesitated again. '…They're evil… Tied up with all sorts of bad men up here…Asian gangs… They're the worst of the lot…They'll do anything and the police don't touch them…I know from Dad…That's why he's so scared…More of the brothers than Mr Khan…They want her and Paul dead… If you can't help them no one can… Meena says that Paul's mum found out about you…You've helped people before…Please do it for Meena…Or if not for her for the baby…The baby never hurt anyone…' She was almost in tears, and I knew what bravery it had been for this girl, not much more than a baby herself, to come to me. And I hoped that if my own daughter went to a stranger and begged for his help that he would help her.

I found my cigarettes in my pocket and lit one, and against my better judgement I cast the die. 'OK,' I said. 'I'll do what I can, but I can't promise.'

Forty-two

'So where is she?' I asked.
'Moving around, from bed and breakfast to bed and breakfast.'

'Where right now? When she phoned you?'

'In a place called Cubitt Town. It sounds funny to me. Do you know it?'

'It's on the Isle of Dogs. East London.' Jesus, I thought. That's where I'd been looking when I went to visit the graves of Dawn, Daisy and Tracey that afternoon after seeing Paul Jeffries' mother. Over to the Isle of Dogs. Maybe Meena had been looking back at me.

'That sounds funny too,' said Caroline. 'Do dogs live there?'

'Long story. I'll tell you one day. Not many dogs, but there's a lot of Asians there.'

'She's running out of places to go. And she says that she stays indoors a lot. Paul does the shopping. When she does go out she wears a veil.'

'Good idea.'

'She wants to meet you,' said Caroline.

'I don't know what I can do. Surely now she's married and pregnant her family will leave her alone, if she tells them.'

'She said it'll be worse.'

'Shit,' I said under my breath. 'When?' I asked out loud.

'As soon as possible.'

'We'll be going back to London tomorrow,' I said. 'I can meet her Monday. You've got my home and office numbers on that card. Give them to her and get one of them to call me.'

'You won't tell her father.'

'Hardly. We didn't part on the best of terms. I ended up nearly giving him a smack. Or one of the brothers, or Rajah, or all of them. But I thought it better to just leave, I've been knocked about enough for now.' I touched my eye. 'No, I won't be telling anyone.'

'Not even if he were to give you a lot of money? He would if he knew.'

'He's already given me a lot of money. I'm going to send most of it back. I promise you Caroline that I won't tell. I don't give my word and then go back on it. Well not often anyway, and not in this case. I'll see Meena and Paul and try to do what I can to help. But tell her when you speak to her, I don't think it'll be much. Why doesn't she get out of the country?'

'She won't go. She says this is where she lives, and this is where she wants her baby to be born. She's stubborn. If she wasn't I doubt if any of this would've happened. Once she set her heart on Paul that was it.'

'Well they've got that in common,' Melanie interjected. 'Meena and Nick. Stubbornness, I mean.'

'She's going to phone me tomorrow,' said Caroline. 'I'll pass on the message.'

'She phones you,' I said. 'At home. Isn't that dangerous?'

'No. I've got my own phone in my room. Daddy bought it for me on my sixteenth birthday. He was tired of the phone downstairs being engaged all the time. And Meena only phones at a prearranged time when I know I'll be there. She only lets it ring twice, then she hangs up.'

'You've been watching too many spy movies,' I said.

'But it works,' she replied. 'I miss her so much. She was my best friend. We just have to talk.'

'Sure you do,' I said. 'And I'm glad she's got a friend like you.'

Caroline smiled. 'Now I'd better get home,' she said. 'I promised I'd be early.'

'And you never break a promise either,' I said.

'Sometimes. But not tonight.'

'Shall I call you a cab?' I asked.

'Better not,' she said. 'I'll go out the back way and find one on the street.'

'You be careful,' I said.

'I always am.' She stood up, put on her coat and went to the door. She hesitated, then ran back, threw her arms round my neck and gave me a wet kiss on the cheek. 'I wish you were my dad,' she said, grinned, then went back to the door, opened it and vanished.

Forty-three

'YOU'VE GOT A fan there,' said Melanie after Caroline had gone. 'So young and pretty too.'

'So many fans, so little time,' I replied. 'But this is no laughing matter. We're talking murder here, and that girl is in danger if anyone finds out she's been talking to Meena.'

'Who's going to find out?'

'Her father?'

'Her own father won't go telling tales.'

'Don't you believe it. I saw him. He's scared shitless. I don't know if it's of losing his job or his life. But whatever it is he'll crack under the slightest pressure.'

'She told you Meena only calls at a certain time when she's by the phone.'

'And how secure is that? She's been lucky so far, but everyone's luck runs out eventually.'

'We've got to pray that hers doesn't. So tell me. What happened at your meeting with the Khans?'

I told her about the face-off I'd had, including the guns. Melanie doesn't like guns. 'Oh Christ,' she said when I got to that part and looked at the door. 'They know where we are.'

'They won't come here.'

'Are you sure?'

'If they're not going to do me serious damage in the privacy of their own restaurant, I doubt if they're going to in a hotel.'

'There is that,' she said, but didn't sound entirely convinced.

'They sound like really bad people,' she said when I'd finished.

'They are. You heard what Caroline said. That's why I'm worried about her. And Meena and Paul and their family and friends. And you and me. This thing's getting out of hand.'

'And I said you'd carry on helping.'

'Good call, babe.'

'I didn't know there would be guns involved.'

'There's always guns when I'm around. It seems I attract them like a magnet.'

'Don't make jokes about it.'

'Who's joking?'

'So what do we do?'

'Go back to London first thing and wait for her call. That's all we can do.'

'And when Meena gets in touch?'

'I'll go and meet her. I don't know what to suggest. She won't go to the cops or the DSS. She won't leave the country. She's pregnant and penniless. However much Paul loves her I don't reckon he'll be much help. Christ, Mel, I'm not often lost for ideas but this time I am.'

'You'll think of something.'

'I bloody well hope so. Those Khan boys are just about capable of anything.'

'Come to bed, love. Get some sleep. We've got an early start.'

'All right.'

So we went to bed, but I hardly slept and when I got the alarm call I'd booked from reception after finding out the time of the first train back to Euston I was still wide awake and staring at the ceiling.

Forty-four

THE NEXT MORNING we slunk out of the hotel like a pair of dogs with their tails between their legs. But once we were on the train I felt better. London was just a pair of silver rails away. I knew where I was in London. At least I thought I did. We travelled first class again. I still had the balance of Khan's money and he could wait for the change. I'd put a jockey on the cheque when I'd paid it into my bank to make sure it cleared fast, and it had.

We ate a massive breakfast and read the Sunday papers on the way down.

It had been raining in Manchester again, but the weather started to clear on the journey and by the time we got close to London the day had brightened considerably.

Once at Euston we cabbed it home and were safely indoors just after lunch.

'So, what do we do now?' asked Melanie as she unpacked my bag and stored the purchases she'd made in Manchester away in my wardrobe.

'Wait. Wait for Meena or Paul Jeffries or Caroline Lees to get in touch. Keep our heads down and see what happens.'

'And if nothing happens?'

'Something will happen, believe me,' I assured her. 'Something always does.'

And of course it did.

The phone rang at seven forty-five as we were watching *Coronation Street*. Melanie was determined to spot the star we'd seen in Khan's restaurant. I dragged the phone into the kitchen as she lowered the volume. 'Mr Sharman,' said a small female voice with a faint northern accent.

'That's me.'

'My name is Meena Jeffries.'

'At last. Hello, Meena.'

'Hello, Mr Sharman. You've been looking for me.'

'That's right.'

'I believe you've fallen out with my family.'

'You might say that.'

'Caroline says I can trust you.'

'As much as you can trust anyone in this wicked world.'

'She says that you can help us.'

'I don't know. I told Caroline that. She has more faith in me than I have in myself, to be honest.'

'We're at our wits' end. We can't run for much longer. You know I'm pregnant.'

'I know.'

'I'm so frightened for my baby.'

'Surely now – now that you're married, your family will accept what you've done.'

'Never.'

'But with a grandchild on the way your father must come round.'

'He means us dead. All of us.' She said it with such dreadful finality I believed her.

'I'm sorry, Meena. I'll help if I can.'

'Can we meet?'

'Of course.'

'You know where I am?'

'Yes. On the Island.'

'There's a park close by. Mudchute, it's called. There's a city farm there. Meet us by the goat enclosure tomorrow at twelve. Can you do that?'

'Sure.'

'You'll come alone?'

'Yes.'

'You won't betray us will you, Mr Sharman? There's three of us now.'

'I won't betray you,' I said.

'You have a kind voice. Caroline said you are a good man. Paul's mother said the same.'

'I'm flattered.' And I was.

'Just don't let us down.'

'I won't,' I said, and I crossed my fingers as I said it. Not to negate the promise, but in the hope that I wouldn't.

She hung up on me then and I listened to the silence at the end of the line before I gently hung up myself.

Forty-five

MONDAY MORNING I got Melanie off to work early, although she was still complaining about being sore from her collision with the dustbins in Manchester's fair city. I could see her angle. She wanted to come along to the Isle of Dogs for the ride, and to meet Meena and Paul. But I was having none of it. I told her that Meena had sounded wary enough at meeting me, and taking someone else might frighten her and Paul off. She argued, but she knew I was right and at last gave in.

'You'll meet them eventually,' I promised her.

I paced the floors of the flat waiting until it was time to leave, drinking coffee and smoking too many cigarettes. Then around quarter to eleven I got fed up with hanging about and got in the Mustang and headed for the East End.

I drove through Camberwell and the Elephant, then took the Rotherhithe Tunnel under the river, turned right into the East India Dock Road and right again at the signs for Canary Wharf with the tower looming over me, its head in the clouds.

If the Thames ran straight at this point, the Isle of Dogs would be in south London and Greenwich and Deptford would be well inland. But instead, the river takes a deep curve southward and leaves the promontory hanging down like the scrotum of north London.

Don't believe me? Then look at the credits for *EastEnders* three times a week on the TV and you'll see.

The island aspect is completed by the fact that the land is almost completely separated from London by water, as the West India and Millwall docks cut across the top, just south of Canary Wharf, and only a few bridges connect it to the rest of the city.

The Isle of Dogs itself is one of the most depressed areas of London, whole swathes of buildings having been flattened during World War Two, followed by more desolation in the 1970s when the docks shut down after containerisation arrived. Then in the 1980s, with the redevelopment of Docklands, the yuppies rolled in with their Beemers and Golfs, and when the recession hit they rolled right out again. Only to reappear with the recovery in the mid-1990s. But the native East Enders stayed put on 'The Island' as they call it as if it was the only one in the world. And to them I suppose it is.

Caroline Lees had asked me if there were dogs there, as if by implication that is how the place got its name. There *are* plenty of dogs around, at least by the amount of dog shit I saw on the pavements as I drove along there are. But that's not it. Not strictly speaking. There are two theories I've heard. The first is that when Charles II lived in Greenwich Palace, it's where he kept his hunting dogs so that he wouldn't be kept awake by their howling at night. The other is that, because of the bend in the river, it was where the bodies of dead dogs were washed up as the tide went out. I tend to go for the former. Let's face it, if dogs' bodies were washed up there, why not cats', or humans' or little bunny rabbits', for that matter.

Still. Everywhere has to have a name. And the Isle of Dogs is as good as any.

Better than a lot in fact.

I'd checked my A-Z before I left home and found that Mudchute Park was off Manchester Road. Coincidence that. And was reached by a number of dead-ended back streets. I parked outside a pub on the corner of one of them at eleven-thirty. I could see the girders of the Millennium Dome sticking up from Blackwall, and knew that if I went a little further down the road to Island Gardens, and walked through the foot tunnel, I could be in Greenwich in a few minutes and visit Dawn, Daisy and Tracey's graves. But I had other fish to fry. I'd do it another time.

I went into the pub, which seemed pleasant enough, for a quick half only to discover two mallards sitting in the bar. Straight up. Two birds of the feathered variety, bold as brass sitting by the bar.

'It'll rain later,' said the barman in answer to my quizzical look at the ducks.

'Fair enough,' I said and left it.

Life's strange enough without making it more difficult by asking silly questions.

Forty-six

I FINISHED MY drink and the cigarette I'd had with it and left the boozer. The two ducks waddled after me, took one look at the sky and decided better of it. I was glad. The last thing I wanted to do was go to my rendezvous accompanied by a pair of our feathered friends.

I walked through the back streets to the entrance to Mudchute Park and city farm and found the goat enclosure by following my nose. It was as ripe as a gone-off cheese and I found a bench facing the paddock where old goats were doing what old goats do, sat down and lit another Silk Cut. It was five to twelve by my Rolex.

I sat and was watching some little nippers throwing bits of food to the goats who snarfed them up big style when someone appeared from a path to my left. It was a woman dressed in a long black jellaba, a black headdress and veil. She wafted towards me and sat down. I looked at her and all I could see were a pair of black, sparkling eyes. I trod out my cigarette. 'Mr Sharman,' she said.

'Meena.'

'You came alone?' Her voice was deep and the accent was pure Manchester.

'Of course.'

She seemed to relax and unhooked the veil. She was beautiful. More beautiful than the photographs I'd seen, with smooth brown skin and lips almost too red and full to be real without collagen injections. 'Good,' she said.

'So we meet at last,' was all I could think to say.

'Shall we walk?' she said.

'By all means.'

We stood and went through a gate into the park and away from the stink of the animals. 'You won't tell my father will you,' she said.

'No. I don't think your father is interested in anything I've got to say.'

'He'd be interested that we met.'

'Yes,' I agreed. 'I think he probably would.'

Suddenly we were joined by a third party. He appeared from behind some bushes and fell into step with us. I recognised Paul Jeffries from the photos, but he appeared much older and his face was tired and lined. 'Paul,' I said. 'How are you?'

'Knackered,' he answered. 'Fed up.' Then to Meena, 'Is he all right?' His accent was south London.

'I'd say so,' she replied. And I realised who was captain of this little craft.

'Thank Christ for that,' said Paul and lit a cigarette without offering me one.

'You two are in danger,' I said.

'Do you think we don't know that?' snapped Paul.

'Paul,' admonished Meena. 'Listen to Mr Sharman.'

'I don't know how to help you,' I said as we stopped at the brow of a low hill and looked out over the island to Greenwich Observatory on our left and Canary Wharf on our right. In front of us a DLR train ran like a toy into Mudchute station.

'Anything,' said Meena.

'Why don't you go abroad?' I asked.

'My baby is British,' said Meena proudly. 'I want him born here.'

'And we've got no dough,' said Paul.

'Where are you living?' I said.

'Over there.' Meena pointed in the general direction of the centre of the island.

I didn't push her. 'Have you got a phone?' I asked.

She shook her head. 'We use a pay phone down the street.'

'Probably the best idea,' I said,

'We can't do anything in our own names,' added Paul. 'Every time we've tried, Meena's father finds out. It's uncanny.'

'He knows a lot of people,' she said.

'Too many,' Paul remarked. 'And we've got no money. I can't get the dole, obviously, so I've picked up a bit of cash cleaning car windscreens in Poplar.'

I felt desperately sorry for the pair of them. 'We've only got a shitty little room to live in. And Meena hasn't been out for a week,' he continued bitterly.

'I daren't,' she cut in. 'I'm so worried someone will recognise me.'

'Are you sure you don't want me to approach your father on your behalf?' I said.

'No,' said Meena, alarmed, and she grabbed my sleeve. 'He won't rest until we're dead.'

'Listen, Meena, Paul,' I said, including him in. 'I understand something of what's happening. But killing you. Are you sure he'd go that far?'

'And further,' said Meena. 'He'd do anything to regain his pride.'

'Listen,' I said, changing the subject and needing time to think. 'Are either of you two hungry?'

'Starving,' they chorused.

'OK. Let's go somewhere and get something to eat. My treat. Or at least it's on your dad, Meena. I've still got plenty of his money.'

'Serves him right,' she said, and we turned round and headed for Manchester Road again, and whatever culinary delights were in store for us there.

Forty-seven

WE WALKED SEPARATELY, so as not to draw attention to ourselves. Paul and me together in front, Meena behind. And we didn't. Draw attention to ourselves, that is. There were several women or groups of women in traditional dress on the streets and we didn't get a second glance.

'She's pregnant and I can't even walk with her,' said Paul bitterly as we went.

'That's tough.'

I saw that he was looking at me as we walked. After a moment's thought he said, 'What happened to your eye?'

'I had a bit of bother,' I replied.

'What happened?'

'I met your brother.'

'Pete?'

'Have you got any others?'

'No.'

'Then that's him.'

'Jesus.'

'And a pair of his workmates.' I didn't want him to think I'd got a beating one to one. 'They weren't happy about me visiting your mum.'

'He's a bloody fool, my brother.'

'You can't blame him for thinking the worst after what Khan's sons did.'

'So what happened?'

'I went to the site where he's working. He came at me with a hammer.'

'And you're still around?' He sounded surprised.

'Just about.'

'I'm really sorry.'

'Not as sorry as they are,' I said.

'You took on three of them?'

'I had no choice. They took me on.'

'And you walked away.'

'Ran, more like.'

'But you won.'

'It wasn't Marquis of Queensberry rules. I fought dirtier than them. I was lucky.'

'Still. Maybe Meena's right to trust you.'

'Thanks,' I said.

'I don't suppose you think much of me, Mr Sharman,' he said after a further short silence.

'I don't know what to think.'

'I suppose Meena's father had plenty to say.'

'Plenty,' I agreed.

'And nothing good.'

'Not a thing.'

'I thought as much.'

'He told me that you sneaked your way into the family to get Meena.'

He laughed without humour. 'Are you kidding? I had it good up there. A steady job, friends. A future. The last thing I wanted was to end up in a mess like this. We couldn't help it. We really tried. But there was something there. Something we couldn't fight. I know. It sounds corny as hell, but it just happens to be true and you can believe it or not.'

'And he told me you'd been inside,' I went on.

'Mr Sharman. I was a kid. I did bad things. Nicking, fighting, skanking people. I ain't proud of it, and if I could go back and change how things were I would. We all make mistakes. I made my share. How about you?'

I couldn't deny that. 'Me too,' I said.

'But now I'm with Meena I'm going straight. Christ knows there's been enough times we haven't had enough to eat and it would've been easy to go on the rob. But she won't have it. She said right at the start that we had to be honest. Well, after we ran away anyway. We couldn't be honest about that. But Jesus, we've paid for it. We've been dumped on, stitched up, lied to, treated like dirt. Treated like criminals, and our only crime was to fall in love. You wouldn't believe it. The DSS let on where we were. Even the cops, though I shouldn't expect any better from them. Believe me, I'm telling you the truth.'

'I believe you,' I said.

He looked surprised. 'Do you? Why?'

'Because of the other people who believe in you.'

'Who's that?'

'Your mum and Meena. Even though I've only met them for a few minutes they seem like good people. And if they trust you...' I didn't finish.

'Thanks, Mr Sharman,' he said. 'I appreciate that.'

We gave the first restaurant we came to, an Indian, a miss. A few doors down was a small Chinese. We went inside. It was empty when we arrived, and it remained empty the whole time we were there.

We took a table at the back partly sheltered by a palm tree plant. Meena unhooked her veil so that she could eat and the waiter gave her a funny look but that was all.

I ordered beer, Paul and Meena had water. I left the food ordering to them and they seemed to want everything on the menu apart from the phone number, and I'm pretty sure that if there'd've been some way to get it down their throats they would've ordered it as well.

'So will you help us?' asked Meena after the waiter had filled three pages of his pad and gone to warn the kitchen that the gannets were in town.

'I'm expensive,' I said.

'How much?' said Paul, with an 'I thought as much' look on his face.

'Got a pound coin?' I asked.

He frowned, reached into the pocket of his denim jacket and brought out a handful of change. He found a pound.

'Give it to me,' I said.

He handed it over.

'I'm hired,' I said.

'For a quid?' said Paul.

'For a quid. For as long as you need me, all expenses paid.' I must've been crazy. 'Now here comes the food.' That shut them up.

The meal wasn't up to much by my standards of Chinese, too much MSG for my taste, but Meena and Paul loved it. Of course they'd gone hungry recently and I hadn't. It's all subjective. Even though it seemed we'd ordered enough for ten we managed to finish the main courses and they still wanted ice cream afterwards. I had a coffee and brandy. The coffee was foul, the brandy not quite so.

'Right,' I said when all plates and dishes were wiped clean. 'I'm going to have to go away and have a think. You know of all the cases I've ever taken on this is the most difficult. I'm buggered if I know what to do.'

'You'll think of something,' Meena said.

Paul nodded agreement.

I had a feeling they were already relying on me to perform miracles.

'You two better go,' I said. 'I'll settle up the bill and have another drink.'

Paul went out first and turned right. Meena waited a minute, clipped her veil up and went after him, turning left. Before she went she put her hand on mine. 'Please do what you can?' she said.

'Give me a couple of days,' I said. 'Then call me.' I offered her money before she went but she refused, even when I told her it was mine, not her father's. She was a proud one all right.

I watched her leave as I sipped at my drink and wondered just what I was letting myself in for, and how come a restaurant could stay open for three hours with only three customers.

I don't remember now to which question I gave the most attention.

Forty-eight

I DROVE BACK to my flat then and phoned Melanie at work and told her what had occurred. 'You be careful,' she said. 'I don't trust any of that lot.'

'I trust Paul and Meena,' I told her. 'Don't ask me why.'

'Is she as good looking as the photograph?' she asked.

I told her she was.

'Then she probably just fluttered her eyelashes at you.'

'Paul didn't, and I trust him too.'

'You south London boys always do stick together.'

'Not always. Remember his brother.'

'So what next?'

'Wait and see. Try and come up with some solution. I tell you, Mel, this is a tough one.'

'When will I see you then?' she asked.

'I thought you'd've had enough after the weekend.'

'Enough of you. No. Not yet.'

'You will let me know though.'

'You'll know. I won't be around.'

'Fair enough. When do you want to see me?'

'How about tonight?'

'You are a glutton for punishment.'

'That's me.'

'Well if you want.'

'I want.'

'OK then. Come round after work.'

'I'll be there.'

'Good.'

We hung up then and I poured a drink and chased the problem of Paul and Meena round inside my head until the doorbell of my flat rang.

I went downstairs to answer, and there on the doorstep were the cops.

Forty-nine

THERE WERE TWO of them. Plainclothes, waving warrant cards. One tall, one short. One with a lot of hair, one with not much. The big one with the hair introduced himself as Sergeant Patterson, the small one without was Detective-Inspector Ramsey. 'Nick Sharman,' said Ramsey. 'We've got a few questions. Mind if we come in?'

I think he'd've liked me to have minded. 'What's it about?' I asked.

'All in good time. And not in public, eh? Top floor isn't it?'

'You've been peeping,' I said.

He cocked his head like a dog with a rabbit in its sights. I pulled open the door and stepped back. 'After you,' said the inspector.

I went up first with the two coppers on my tail. All the way up I wondered what the hell this was all about and what I had in the flat that could be used against me.

When we got inside the door, Patterson closed it behind him and Ramsey looked round. 'Nice,' he said. 'A little palace.'

'Can we get to the point, Inspector?' I said. 'What do you want? Not interior design tips, surely.'

He sat down on the sofa and opened his jacket as if he was in for a long stay. Patterson took one of the stools by the breakfast bar. 'Do sit down, Mr Sharman,' said Ramsey. 'You're making me nervous.'

Of course truth to tell it was me with the nerves. He looked as comfortable as could be sitting there in front of me. I shrugged and sat on the only chair.

'You see, what it is Mr Sharman is that we're the Old Bill and our job for the next few minutes is to ask you some questions, and your job is to answer them. Get me?'

Amusing geezer, I thought and opened my mouth to make some smart remark, but he held up his hand to silence me. 'Stop right there for a few seconds before you answer in the negative, and let me explain further. Because we know all about you, son. We know your predilection for big boys' toys.

Guns and suchlike. You see the way it is we can do this here all friendly like and you can tell us exactly what you know and part on good terms. *Or...*' and he emphasised the word, 'we can do it down the station and that means we get a warrant to spin this place, and God knows what we'll find. Because we can. And there's other things we've heard about you isn't there, Sergeant?'

'We heard you're a dope fiend,' said the hirsute sergeant.

'A dope fiend,' repeated the inspector. 'Now that's not an expression you hear too often these days is it, Mr Sharman? Junkie is the word we use now. But dope fiend will do. So tell me. If we did give this place a going over what do you think we'd find?'

'Something that wasn't here when you started,' I ventured.

'Very good. You must've been taught well when you were on the drug squad. Always bring something to the party yourself. A good motto. What do you say, Sergeant?'

The sergeant nodded and grunted.

'See. Think of all the time and aggro you'd save all of us if you just cooperate right from the get-go. A couple of hours for us and maybe as much as ten years for yourself. It's like the old saying: 'For want of a horse the battle was lost.' Only in your case it's more like: 'For the want of a little chat your arse is mine.' So what's it to be?'

'I'll cooperate,' I said.

'Maybe you could make us some tea while we're here. It's thirsty work chatting,' the inspector said with a mean smile.

What had I got to lose? Only my freedom. 'OK,' I said and got up to put on the kettle.

'Got any bikkies?' he added. 'Digestive's favourite. Got any digestive, have you?'

'I might be able to find some,' I said.

'Milk chocolate, I hope.'

'Milk chocolate,' I echoed.

'See,' he said, sitting back with a big smile on his chops. 'We're getting along like a house on fire already. We even share the same taste in tea-time snacks.'

Fifty

WHILST I WAS preparing the tea things and finding the biscuit tin, I was trying to work out exactly why these two were here. I'd been a good boy lately, and apart from the pistol hidden in the roof outside my flat door I was as clean as clean. Not that that doesn't mean a couple of years in the chokey, no danger. But it wasn't exactly *in* the flat and no one had ever found the little hidey-hole I keep it in before, so I wasn't that worried. Maybe there were a few traces of spliff scattered about inside, but it would take a sniffer dog with a very keen nose to find even that.

I put everything on a tray like a proper little ladies' tea party and when the kettle was boiled made the drinks.

'Cheers,' said Ramsey when I handed him his. Patterson just grunted. Manners, I thought.

When we were all happy with our refreshments Ramsey said round a mouthful of chocolate biscuit, 'So what have you been up to lately, Mr Sharman? Or may I call you Nick?'

'Mr Sharman will do,' I replied.

'Formal,' said Ramsey, obviously enjoying himself immensely. 'That's good.'

'I like to keep things formal,' I agreed.

'Best way. So? Tell us all?'

'Nothing much to tell,' I replied.

'Earning a crust?'

'You might say that.'

'Got a new girlfriend too. Quite a looker from what I hear.'

'You must've had your ear close to the ground.'

'That's what I do, isn't it, sergeant?' he said. 'Keep my ears close to the ground.'

Patterson grunted again and surveyed the inside of his mug as if looking for the meaning of life.

I took out my cigarettes.

'Don't mind if I do,' said Ramsey.

I threw one to him. He reminded me of another copper I knew of the same rank. DI Robber. Or to be exact ex-DI

Robber who had helped me in a few cases since his retirement and ended up the worse for it. He never smoked his own fags either.

'My sergeant thinks it's a filthy habit,' Ramsey said, accepting a light. 'But it's one of my very few pleasures.'

Alongside giving recalcitrant interviewees a good bashing, I thought, but didn't vocalise it.

'So tell me about Meena Khan,' he said.

I was so surprised I almost corrected him about her surname, but bit my tongue just in time. So that was it, and me knowing she was married would put me right in it.

'Who?' I said.

'Oh don't,' he said. 'No. Don't insult my intelligence. Meena Khan. Inamorata of Paul Jeffries. You're looking for them.'

'Was,' I corrected him. 'In the past tense. No longer. I resigned.'

'That's not what we heard.'

'Then you heard wrong. And that's what this is about, is it? You're taking the piss, aren't you? Jesus, I might've known. You come in here threatening beatings and search warrants and trips down the station and all sorts. And what it really is, is this is your part-time job. You're bought and paid for, aren't you? This is freelance, right? How much did it cost Khan for a home visit? What's the callout charge?'

'Don't know the man,' said Ramsey.

'But someone does, don't they?' I said. 'Someone you owe a favour to. Bloody hell I thought all this had stopped.'

'All what?' Patterson chimed in.

'Backhanders. Interviews without benefit of PACE,' I said.

'When did you think it stopped then?' Patterson asked. 'When they threw you out of the force? Don't you believe it, Sharman. We're here for information and we mean to get it.'

'You going to knock it out of me?'

'If we have to,' said Patterson.

'Not so fast, Sergeant,' interrupted Ramsey. 'I don't think that will work. Anyway it looks like someone already tried it.'

I touched my face, almost by force of habit by then.

'No,' the DI continued. 'We're going to leave Mr Sharman to think about it. To think how difficult we can make his life in the future. No beatings. No Gestapo tactics. Just consider, Mr Sharman. You do what you do with our consent. And by our, I mean the forces of law and order, from traffic wardens to Her Majesty's Department of the Inland Revenue. We leave you alone to carry on your sleazy little business as you want. But if we put a magnifying glass to your life I bet we'd come up with all sorts. And we can. Believe me we can.

'You're right. We owe a few faces a few favours. Important faces. And they want to collect. So, we'll leave you now, but we'll be back. Tomorrow evening I think, and we'll want some answers. And by then I think you'll be in a position to supply them. Otherwise…Well otherwise doesn't bear thinking about, does it?' He got to his feet and Patterson did the same. 'So until then Mr Sharman it's *au revoir*. Not goodbye.'

And they left, leaving only the dregs in the mugs and a few biscuit crumbs behind.

'Shit!' I said aloud after they'd gone. 'Shit! Shit! Shit!'

Fifty-one

MELANIE ARRIVED AT six-thirty. By that time I was walking the floor. 'What's up?' she said.

'I've had the police here.'

'*What?*'

'The Met's finest. A couple of chancers earning a back-hander by giving me a hard time.'

'What about?'

'What do you think? Or rather who. Meena and Paul of course. Khan's pulling a few strings.'

'Do they know you've seen them?'

'Not for sure. But the hounds have got the scent and they're moving in.'

'Oh *Nick*.'

'Oh *Melanie*.'

'You don't seem to be treating this very seriously.'

'Don't you believe it. It's serious all right. The Bill are threatening all sorts of nasty sanctions. And a good smacking as well of course.'

'Can't you do anything?'

'Like what? Go to the police complaints board? I don't think so. I can hear them laughing up their sleeves from here.'

'I wish you'd never got into this, Nick.'

'So do I. But whose bright idea was it that I got into the real world?'

'Mine. I'm sorry.'

'Don't be. I make my own decisions. Well, mostly anyway.'

'So what about these police?'

'They're coming back tomorrow for some answers. And if I don't come up with any I think I'm going to take a little ride with them. Them and a couple of rubber hoses.'

'Don't, Nick, you're scaring me.'

Truth to tell I was scaring myself. 'Don't worry,' I said. 'I don't intend to be here.'

'But you can't run for ever.'

'Sounds like a line from one of those films you like to watch in the middle of the night. Van Johnson is it? Or George Montgomery?'

She shook her head. 'What am I going to do with you?' she asked.

'I dunno. I just wish Meena or Paul would call.'

But of course they didn't. No one did.

That night was a pivotal one for Melanie and me. It was the night that I felt her begin to slip away. Slip through my fingers like sand as so many other women had done.

She slapped a couple of frozen pasta meals from Marks & Sparks into the microwave and opened a bottle of red wine she'd brought with her. It was cool from the air outside and refreshing. I sipped at it as I watched her set the table. 'Sorry,' I said. 'I'd've done that, but I thought we might go out.'

'Not tonight, Nick,' she said. 'And besides, I want to talk.'

Why did those last six words bring dread to my heart?

When the food was hot she served it and we sat down. I was watching the phone as if somehow, by concentrating I could make it ring. But it remained silent.

'Have you ever thought about having more children, Nick?' was Melanie's opening salvo.

Fuck me, I thought. Where the hell did *that* one come from? Tonight of all nights. I tried not to choke on my food as I answered. 'Not really,' I said. 'Why?'

'Just a thought. You know it's my birthday next month.'

And the old biological clock's ticking, I thought. 'Yeah,' I said.

'I'm not getting any younger.'

'Nor are any of us.'

'It's just that sometimes…'

'You feel the need to breed.' Not a particularly sensitive thing to say, I'll admit.

'When you put it like that…'

'Sorry. But this is all a bit of a surprise. Apart from your approaching birthday what's brought it on?'

'Being away over the weekend. Being together.'

'We're together now.'

She sighed. 'Until tomorrow when I go back to work.'

'You want to give up work, is that it?'

'We could manage.'

'*We*, White man,' I said.

'You don't like the idea of "we"?'

'Melanie,' I said after a sip of wine which was warming in the room. 'I've got one child. A grown-up now. Who I hardly ever see. I've got another in a grave not many miles from here. Both their mothers are dead. I'm not exactly an actuary's dreamboat. Women don't have a long shelf life round me.'

I was trying to be flippant but it wasn't working. Not for Melanie and certainly not for me. I'd spent too many sleepless nights wondering what if? What if I'd been a better husband to my first wife Laura, what if I'd kept my second wife, Dawn out of harm's way and not involved her in a particularly nasty case involving drug smugglers? Too much guilt to be flippant. 'I don't know if I can take the risk of long term commitment again. I'm not a young bloke any more. I've got too much baggage. Too many bad memories. And right now, after today's visit from the thin blue line I don't even know if I'll have my freedom for much longer.' Why do women have to bring up this sort of subject at the most inopportune time?

'I know, Nick. But I watched you with Caroline in that hotel room. You've also got a lot of love to give. It would be too bad to see that turn to bitterness as you grow old alone.'

'Who says I'm going to grow old? And I sometimes think I'm meant to be alone.'

'No one is.'

'There's always someone.'

'You see I'd like a child, Nick, and God help me I'd like you to be the father.'

'You can certainly pick 'em.'

'I picked you the first day we met. Remember? At that restaurant?'

'How can I forget. You were gagging for it.'

'I hate that expression.'

'I know. That's why I used it.'

'We're good together, Nick.'

'We are,' I agreed. 'But it's a big step.'

'A step you don't want to make. Is that what you mean?'

'Not necessarily.'

'But you're not exactly putting out the flags.'

I had to agree I wasn't. 'And if the answer's no?' I said.

'Then what we were talking about on the phone may happen.'

'You not being here, you mean?' I said.

'That's about it.'

I felt that old cold hand on my heart again. 'Do I have to give you an answer right away?' I asked.

'Of course not. It's a big step like you said. I've been thinking about it and so should you.'

'I will,' I promised.

'Just don't take too long. I'm not a young maiden any more.'

'And I'm not exactly the answer to a young maiden's prayer,' I replied.

'You can say that again,' she said, and we both laughed. But the laughter had a hollow ring about it.

Fifty-two

WE WENT TO bed reasonably early but didn't make love. That seemed to be happening more and more lately. I know she had her period, but that had never stopped us before. Like I said, Melanie was slipping away, as a lot of other things seemed to be doing that autumn night when the leaves dropped softly to the pavements and the streetlights were haloed with gold.

The next morning she went off to work, giving me just a perfunctory kiss on the cheek and me giving her the perfunctory promise of a call soon. Somehow things had changed, and I knew they could never be the same again. But we both put a brave face on it as if nothing had happened. 'Be careful,' she said as she walked through the door, her only reference to my troubles. Seemed like I was on my own now.

But then that was nothing new.

I spent the rest of the day in the flat waiting for Paul or Meena to call and wondering what to do about avoiding Detective-Inspector Ramsey and Sergeant Patterson.

In fact I only got one call all day. It was from Paul's mate Henry. 'I've got some news,' he said.

'What kind of news?' I asked. The way things were going it could only be bad.

'About Paul and Meena.'

'What about them?'

'Not on the phone,' he said. 'Can we meet?'

'Do you know where they are?' I pressed. If he did, there was a chance a lot of others did too. Including the cops, maybe.

'I told you, not on the phone. I need to see you.'

'Fair enough,' I said, but I wasn't happy. 'When?'

'Tonight.'

It was my night for rendezvous obviously. 'What time?'

'Eight o'clock, at the same place.'

'I'll be there,' I said, and he hung up, leaving me looking at the dead phone in my hand and wondering just exactly what the hell was going on.

I left the house early and went for something to eat, although I had no appetite and it was just to kill time and avoid the law. Eventually it was time for my appointment with Henry and I drove to Streatham Common again.

He was sitting by the bar when I arrived and I joined him. He seemed nervous and was sucking on a cigarette like it was going to be his last. 'Hi Henry,' I said. 'What's up?'

When he saw me he reached for his pint and nearly knocked it flying. 'Calm down, son,' I said. 'It's too expensive to waste.'

'Sorry,' he replied.

'Want another?' I said.

'Sure. Lager.'

I ordered a couple of pints and whilst we were waiting for them I said, 'So what have you got for me?'

He looked round nervously. 'Let's talk in the back,' he said.

I paid for the drinks, picked up mine and we went into the little back bar which was empty. We sat down and Henry lit another cigarette. 'So?' I said. 'You've got something to tell me.' If it was the fact that Paul and Meena were on the Isle of Dogs it was old news. But if it was their actual address I was more than interested.

'Someone wants to see you,' he said.

'Who?'

He looked towards the door of the bar and my eyes followed his, half expecting Ramsey and Patterson to be on the premises. Or even Meena and Paul themselves. But instead, standing there grinning, were Peter Jeffries and his two mates from the building site, Yellow and Blue Hat. Except of course, this being after working hours, they were bareheaded. 'Thanks a lot, Henry,' I said. 'This is all I fucking need.'

The trio came into the bar and over to our table. 'We meet again,' said Peter Jeffries like someone out of a spaghetti western.

'Is this it?' I said to Henry. 'How much was I worth?'

'A pony,' said Jeffries. 'Cheap at twice the price.' And he took Henry's cigarette out of his mouth and dropped it into my glass where it hissed as it went out.

'Mulled ale,' I said. 'My favourite.'

'Time to take a walk, Sharman,' said Jeffries. 'We've got business to finish.'

'Remember what happened last time,' I said and winked at him.

'We're ready for you this time,' he replied.

'And if I don't want to go?'

'Then we'll do you here.'

Blue Hat pulled a gravity knife from his pocket and let it drop open with an oily click.

'All right, all right, I'm coming,' I said.

'You too, Henry,' said Peter as I got up and they hustled me across the floor into the main bar and towards the front door, Jeffries on my left, Blue Hat on my right, his knife hidden in the folds of his long jacket and Yellow Hat and Henry close behind. I knew if they got me outside I was in for a kicking. I wasn't going to get the better of them for a second time in a straight fight.

As we got to the front door it opened and we met two good-looking girls coming in. 'Ladies,' I said and grabbed one and shoved her at Jeffries.

'Oi,' she screamed. 'What the—' But I was gone, out to the front of the pub, taking a hard right and right again in the direction of my car, the door slamming behind me.

I skidded into Greyhound Lane and not ten yards in front of me, standing in the middle of the pavement was a massive figure. The silhouette reminded me of someone I recognised but it couldn't be. Then I realised it was. All neat in shiny suit and turban, there in front of me blocking my escape was Rajah. 'Oh shit,' I said as I skidded to a halt in front of him. 'If you want a piece of me you'd better get in the queue.'

'Having trouble, Mr Sharman?' he said as my pursuers rounded the corner behind me. 'You do seem to attract it.'

'What the fuck—' I said, but he brushed me aside like a gnat as Peter Jeffries and his posse came tumbling after me.

I half expected them to be in it together, but I was proved wrong as Rajah swung a mighty fist into Jeffries' face and dropped him like a stone to the ground. Blue Hat was right on his tail, his knife in clear view and Rajah caught his hand, crushing the handle in his fist with the unmistakable sound of breaking bones. Using Blue Hat's own momentum he swung him up and over the fence of the house we were in front of, where he landed with a crash on top of a metal dustbin. Rajah pivoted on his toes with incredible grace for such a huge man and smashed his elbow into the throat of Yellow Hat, who was coming up hard behind him, without missing a beat, and left my third assailant gasping and choking on the floor next to Peter Jeffries. Henry had stopped at the sight of the carnage and was trying to backpedal away when Rajah grabbed him by his short hair and shoved him out into the street where he hit the side of a passing bus and bounced back, tripping over the kerb and going full length on to the pavement face first.

The whole incident had only taken a second or two but people were stopping and the bus had halted at the lights. I could see faces peering back at us from inside.

'Come on,' said Rajah who was not even out of breath. 'Let's go.'

'My car—' I said

'Not that thing. Leave it. Mine's down there.' The Mercedes was parked twenty or thirty yards down a side street out of sight, facing towards us. 'Come on before the police arrive.'

We legged it across the street past the small crowd that had gathered, down to where the car was waiting. Rajah slid behind the wheel and I jumped into the front passenger seat as he started the motor and headed down Greyhound Lane in the direction of Mitcham. 'We've got to get another car,' he said. 'Someone's bound to have got the number of this one.'

'Where did you come from?' I asked. 'And what's going on?'

'Why don't you ask them?' he said and pointed a thumb behind him. I looked into the back seat, and there, wide eyed and as quiet as two mice, were Paul and Meena.

Fifty-three

I LOOKED AT them with what must have been much the same amazement that I'd shown when I saw Rajah waiting outside the pub. Or when Peter Jeffries and his mates turned up inside. Or for that matter when the police arrived on my doorstep. Lately, I think I'd spent an inordinate amount of time looking amazed. 'What the…?' I said.

Meena was now dressed in jeans and a sweater with her face uncovered, and she wore an 'I'm sorry' expression.

I put two and two together fast. 'He's on your side,' I said, looking at Rajah.

Meena nodded.

'Terrific,' I said. 'There's nothing like trust between a detective and his clients. You might've told me.'

'We couldn't tell you,' said Meena. 'Not right away. Not until we were sure we could trust you absolutely.'

'So what's all this about?' I demanded. 'What makes you so sure you can trust me now?'

'You were followed,' interrupted Rajah. 'That bloody stupid car of yours sticks out like a sore thumb.'

'Who followed me?' I asked.

'Some friends of my father's,' said Meena.

'And Rajah heard.'

'That's right,' Rajah said.

'So did the cops,' I said.

'What?' demanded Rajah.

'They were on my doorstep yesterday afternoon. After I saw you two,' I added for Paul and Meena's benefit. And Rajah's.

'What did they want?' asked Paul.

'What do you think? Your whereabouts.'

'You didn't tell them?' said Meena fearfully.

'No. Even though they threatened me with all sorts. I couldn't tell them anyway. The Isle of Dogs is a big place. I had no idea where you were staying.'

'Good,' said Rajah.

'And you came down to warn them when you heard I'd been spotted,' I said to him.

'I had to. I couldn't let those two brothers of hers beat me to it. I collected them last night from where they were staying. Thanks to you it was blown.' Rajah seemed much more articulate now than he had in Manchester.

'Where did you stay last night then?' I asked.

'A B&B in Victoria.' Rajah again.

'So why are you here?'

'Just as well we were,' said Rajah. 'Otherwise that bloke might've cut you a new arsehole. Sorry, Meena.'

'It was your brother and his mates,' I said to Paul. 'Looking for revenge for the whacking I gave them. Henry sold me out.'

'Sorry,' said Paul.

'I think they've all lived to regret it. Rajah broke some bones.'

'And we'll regret it if the police got the number of this car,' interrupted Rajah. 'We need fresh wheels.'

'No,' I said. 'Not necessarily. You got any tools?'

'In the boot,' replied Rajah.

By this time we were in the Mitcham one way system. 'Pull into that pub,' I said.

'We haven't got time to stop for a drink,' said Rajah.

'I know that. Just park up a minute.'

He did as he was told and when we stopped at the dark end of the car park I said, 'Paul, Rajah. Out.'

They both complied and I got Rajah to open the boot and I dug three screwdrivers out of the box of tools he had in there. 'Paul. You get the plates off the car. Rajah, we need a motor with the same year reg. Come on Paul, don't hang about. You must've done this before.'

Rajah and I, armed with a screwdriver each, walked through the car park until we came across a P-reg Volvo. He took the front and I took the rear and within a minute we had the plates off and I took them back to Paul who was waiting with the Merc's registration. 'Put these on,' I said, handing him the Volvo's plates and taking the Merc's in exchange.

'We'll get these on the other motor.'

'Just dump 'em,' he said.

'I thought you'd know better,' I said. 'The driver probably

won't notice that his plates have changed, but he might notice he's got none at all. Now get on with it.'

I stuck the Merc's plates under my jacket and went back to the Volvo where Rajah and I had them on the car in a moment.

'Come on,' I said. 'Quick, before they catch us.'

We legged it back to the Mercedes and within a second or two were on our way. 'Where we going now?' I asked.

'I've borrowed a place. A cottage,' said Rajah.

'Where?' I asked.

'Near Rainy Town,' he replied.

'Manchester!'

'Why not. Now, how the hell do I get back on to the motorway?'

'It's a step,' I said, and pointed to one of the off roads from the system. 'Up there, and keep going. You can drop me off anywhere. I'll get a cab back to my car.'

'You aren't going anywhere,' said Rajah. 'Except with us.'

'Give me a break,' I said. 'I'm out of this now.'

Then I felt a hand on my shoulder and I looked back straight into Meena's limpid black eyes which sparkled from the reflection of the oncoming cars' headlights. 'Please Mr Sharman,' she said. 'Please come with us.'

'Meena,' I pleaded. 'Why do you need me? You've got Rajah.'

'Because you said you'd help. And we did pay you, didn't we?'

'A quid,' I said dismissively and I should've known better.

'And you told us it was for as long as we needed you, expenses paid. Remember?'

I remembered, and I knew I should've kept my mouth shut at the time. Big man trying to impress a couple of kids. Big mug punter, more like. 'I remember,' I said.

'Well we still need you. And a promise is a promise, isn't it?'

'Yes,' I agreed. 'A promise is a promise.'

'Well then,' she said, and sank back into her seat.

There was no answer to that.

'No chance of going back to mine to get a few things, I suppose,' I said to Rajah.

'No. You never know who's waiting.'

I thought of Ramsey and Patterson and had to agree. 'Yeah, I guess you're right. Follow the signs to Balham, then Clapham, and we go over Chelsea Bridge. The motorway's signposted from the West End.'

Fifty-four

IT TOOK US hours to get up north, what with stops for petrol and something to eat at a wind-blown service station somewhere in the Midlands, miles from civilisation, staffed by what seemed to be extras from *The Invasion of the Bodysnatchers*. And all that was after having to listen to Rajah's taste in music for the entire drive.

Inside the cafeteria I picked at some cod, chips and peas in batter that seemed to have some kinship in texture and colour with a damp cardboard box. The fish appeared to have last seen the sea when Britain ruled the waves, the chips only had a nodding acquaintance with *pommes de terre* and the peas you could have loaded into a Colt .45 in mistake for brass-coated bullets. The tea was cold and the ketchup was warm, but as I had little appetite it made no difference. Rajah chose a chicken casserole which he gave up as a lost cause halfway through, and Paul and Meena just ate everything in sight as usual.

'Where is this place you've borrowed?' I asked when we'd finished eating, or in my case pushing the unappetising mess round my plate.

'A little village this side of Manchester,' he replied.

'Who owns it?'

'A mate.'

'Asian?'

'No.'

'A little village you say.'

He nodded affirmation.

'Big Asian community?'

'No.'

'So we'll stick out a bit.'

'If anyone sees us,' he replied.

'They'll see us. People in little villages do that sort of thing. See strangers, I mean.'

'Then we'll have to keep our heads down.'

'For how long?'

Rajah shrugged.

'Like years?' I asked a bit sarcastically. 'I've got a life, you know.'

'I dunno,' said Rajah. 'I just had to get them somewhere safe.'

Meena and Paul had been following our two-handed conversation like spectators at a tennis match, their eyes flicking back and forth between us. Eventually Meena said, 'We are here you know.'

'Sorry,' I replied. 'But it just seems we're getting nowhere fast.'

'And I can't keep running,' she continued. 'I've got the baby to think of.'

'It's a bit late for that.' I was tired and could feel myself getting tetchy.

'You're impossible,' she said. 'I'm going to the Ladies,' and with that she pushed her chair back and flounced off in the direction of the sign that pointed to the toilets.

'She gets her temper off her family,' said Paul by way of apology. 'She's grateful really.'

'And pregnant,' I said. 'Pregnancy does that.'

We sat in silence and cogitated on the ways of women, and on that subject I borrowed Rajah's mobile phone and went outside to phone Melanie at her place.

I told her some, not all of the story.

'Where are you?' she demanded.

'On a far distant galaxy by the looks of it,' I replied as I shivered in the chilly wind that kicked rubbish round the car park of the services and the traffic thumped past on the way back and forth between London and the north.

'When will you be back?'

'Christ knows. This is just a big mess.'

'What are you going to do?'

'I don't know.'

'Well, let me know when you do,' and she hung up on me.

I stood and lit a cigarette and looked at the orange glow on the horizon from the lights of what I supposed was Birmingham where normal people were doing normal things, and I don't think I'd ever felt more alone in my whole life.

Fifty-five

WE LEFT THE services just after midnight and the motorway was pretty quiet except for the HGVs heading in both directions and the occasional private car. 'How much longer?' I said to Rajah, but he just shrugged in return. He put his foot down and moved over to lane three and I saw the needle on the speedometer swing round from 70 to 80 to 90 then over the ton to settle at 120, and that was the speed we were doing when we passed the cop car that was parked on one of those humps on the far side of the breakdown lane.

I saw the blues start to rotate and heard the twin tones as the Rover came after us. 'Shit,' I said, 'we've got company.' Rajah just grunted and put his foot down harder on the accelerator. 'Oh good,' I said. 'A car chase, as if we're not in enough trouble already.'

Rajah looked over his shoulder and said, 'Kids, put on your belts and do them up tight.'

Jesus, I thought. I wonder how fast this baby can go, as the speedo hit 140 without any effort from the big engine and kept climbing.

But the police driver persevered and although he dropped back slightly he was still with us, and of course he had the advantage of a radio and just about as many other squad cars as were within range and fancied a bit of an adventure.

Then Rajah got tired of the chase and decided to make things more interesting. Without warning he slammed on the brakes so hard that the Mercedes' tyres shrieked and threw smoke. By design the ABS kept us in a straight line skid but I didn't know what the hell he was playing at. 'What the...?' I shouted and just as suddenly he let off the brakes, smashed his right foot on to the accelerator and pulled the steering wheel sharply down to the left so that the big car went into a spin across all three lanes before heading back in the direction we'd been coming from directly at the police Rover and two massive articulated lorries that were trundling up the slow and middle lanes, blocking them completely as the police car overtook them, three sets of headlights aimed directly at us, airbrakes hissing and horns braying with seemingly nowhere for us to go. Meena was screaming, Paul was screaming, and I felt like screaming too as we accelerated towards the three vehicles approaching us as if Rajah was determined to commit suicide by smashing into one of them. I was holding on to the grab handle over the passenger door and I almost covered my eyes with my free hand as Rajah straddled the fast lane, aimed over two tons of steel and rubber at the oncoming emergency vehicle and slammed his boot down so hard on the accelerator that I thought his foot would go right through the floor of the Merc. I could see the faces of the coppers in the Rover, both their mouths open in terror. The driver had only one choice. He pulled the car on to the edge of the fast lane and the Rover dragged along the central barrier in a shower of sparks. Rajah just twitched the wheel sufficiently so that we passed between the police car and the HGV in the middle lane and shot down lane three in the wrong direction at more than 150 miles per hour.

I've got to tell you that was a close call, but Rajah didn't turn a hair.

The motorway was lit up like a Christmas tree at that point and Rajah slowed until he found a gap in the central reservation and pulled through it flattening some plastic bollards and we were heading back towards London.

'Jesus Christ,' I said. 'You nearly killed us.'

He just shook his head, pulled into the slow lane and took the next off-ramp up to a roundabout and an A-road that was signposted to Manchester. 'I think we'd better keep off the motorway for now,' was all he said.

I looked into the back where Paul and Meena were sitting wrapped in each other's arms with terrified looks on their faces. 'You can relax now,' I said with a tremor in my voice. 'I think we're going to be OK.'

And we were as we drove on the unlit minor roads with only the moon for company for the hour and a half it took us to get to the village, which of course was unsullied by street lamps, road signs and any other civilised means of finding one's way around so that it took us another half-hour to locate the cottage. Not that it was a big village, it wasn't. But big enough, with sufficient lanes and dead ends to fox even Sherlock Holmes. And of course we couldn't ask anyone. Not that there was anyone on the streets – pardon my exaggeration, what passed for streets – in the boonies we found ourselves, to ask. It was early to bed with your mum, dad, brother and sister in these parts by the looks of it. And I guessed if you had no immediate family, a sheep or two would do.

I hate the fucking country.

But eventually we found the place we were looking for. Rose Cottage it was called, and as far as location was concerned it seemed to be perfect, being at the end of a winding lane with no other dwelling for a quarter of a mile. Rajah pulled into the empty drive, turned off the engine and slid the gear stick of the Mercedes into PARK.

I looked into the back where Meena and Paul had fallen asleep with their heads close together. 'Hansel and Gretel,' I said.

Rajah and I got out of the motor, he found a key under an upturned flower pot and we let ourselves in. Trusting souls in the country.

It was cold and dark inside and smelt of damp. The electricity was off, but with the aid of my Zippo I found the mains box and flicked on the master switch. The cottage was small. Downstairs at the front was the living room, with a dusty three-piece suite, a couple of chairs, a table, and an antique TV set. On the table was an old-fashioned, circular dial telephone. I picked it up and got a dialling tone. Past the living room door, a narrow hall ran down to the kitchen at the back which contained a none too clean electric stove, a turned-off fridge with the door open, and a cupboard with some tea bags, half a packet of sugar and a tin of dried milk. Upstairs were three bedrooms, one double at the back and two singles at the front. The beds were bare. In the fourth corner was a bathroom and toilet with a cold airing cupboard that housed a motley collection of bed linen, blankets and four stained pillows. All the comforts of home.

I was glad of the extra room. I hadn't been looking forward to sharing with Rajah.

There were the makings of a fire in the fireplace in the living room and I found a pile of soggy wood outside the kitchen door at the back and soon got a smoky blaze going, and more logs drying in the hearth.

'Better get them inside,' I said.

Rajah went out to the car and he came back with our two sleepy and yawning charges.

'There's sheets, blankets and pillows in the cupboard in the bathroom,' I said. 'They're a bit cold and damp, but we'll survive. Meena and Paul, you take the big room at the back. Rajah and I'll have the ones in the front. Does anyone want a drink before we turn in?'

Meena and Paul declined but Rajah opted for a cuppa.

I put the kettle on and the other three went upstairs to get their beds organised. Rajah came back alone as I finished making the tea. 'Only dried milk I'm afraid,' I said.

'It doesn't worry me. I drink mine black. But we'd better get some supplies tomorrow.'

'Got any money?' I asked.

'Plenty.'

'Thank Christ for that. I haven't. And from what I gather, going to a hole in the wall will only let Khan know where we've been.'

'There's lots of Indian guys work in banks,' he said.

'What about supermarkets with a credit card?'

'Risky.'

'So I'm in your hands. And talking of hands, it was you, wasn't it?' I said as I put the cups on the draining board.

'What?'

'The car in Manchester. The one that nearly ran me and Melanie down.'

'It was just to frighten you off.'

'Didn't work, did it?'

'It was worth a punt.'

'You could've killed us.'

'No. You've seen me drive. If I'd wanted to kill you I would've.'

I punched him then. A good right to the jaw that seemed to have about as much effect as punching an elephant. Except that I popped a knuckle.

'Shit!' I yelled, putting my injured hand under my arm. 'What've you got? An iron jaw?'

Rajah smiled. 'I guess I owe you that. But next time I'll hit you back, so be warned.'

I looked at his mighty hands and *was* warned. 'Fair enough,' I said.

'Let's have a look,' he said.

Gingerly I held out my hand and he took it in his and popped the knuckle right back. 'You'll be all right,' he said. I suppose in a way it was a gesture of friendship. At least I took it as such.

'Thanks. I suppose I will,' I replied.

'I'm glad you're here,' he said.

'Are you?'

He nodded.

'You never gave me that impression when we were driving around Manchester those couple of days.'

'I thought you were just a poofy southerner.'

'Cheers. What changed your mind?'

'That night in the restaurant with Deepak and Sanjay when they pulled out their guns and you just walked away.'

'I was shitting myself.'

'It didn't show.'

'You don't do my laundry.'

He laughed out loud at that. 'You should've seen their faces. And when you put the chair through the door they didn't know what was going on.'

'I thought they might shoot.'

'Not without Daddy's permission.'

'Well thank Christ for small mercies.'

'I've told you about him before.' Then he picked up his cup and said, 'You coming in to drink your tea in front of the fire?'

Fifty-six

WHEN WE'D FINISHED our drinks Rajah said, 'Come outside, I've got something you should see.'

He took the torch and we went out into the chilly air to the Merc. He opened the boot and the interior light popped on. Inside was the usual stuff. Spare wheel, tool box, spare pair of trainers, a couple of old magazines. Nothing unusual there. Plus an old rolled up tartan blanket. He gave me the torch and unrolled it. 'Fuck me,' I said when I saw what had been wrapped up inside. There were two 9mm semi automatics, a Glock and a Browning, spare clips and a box of ammunition. But what really caught my eye was a Uzi Desert Eagle .44 with a foot-long suppressor screwed to the barrel, a laser sight mounted on top lying next to an AK47 with a banana clip. 'Fuck me,' I said again. 'We going to war?'

'Maybe,' said Rajah. 'But whatever, I like to be prepared.'

'Regular little Boy Scout, ain'tcha,' I said back. 'How are you on knots?'

'Do what?' he asked. Obviously he'd never been one of the Rover boys like me.

'Never mind,' I said. 'No wonder you didn't want those traffic police to flag us down. And there's me just thinking you were overreacting. We've been driving around with stolen plates and these in the back. We *would've* looked good if we'd got a pull.'

'I *never* get pulled.' He sounded quite hurt at the idea.

'Maybe not in Madchester,' I said. 'But we were on the open road. We'd've all ended up in the clink.'

He slammed the boot lid. 'No we wouldn't,' he said chillingly and I knew that if we hadn't lost those cops they wouldn't have lived to see morning. I was glad Rajah was on our side.

'Aren't we going to take them inside?' I asked.

He shrugged. 'They'll be all right here. I don't want Meena to see them. She doesn't like guns.'

'Fair enough,' I said and we went back inside.

When I eventually got to my room and made up the bed, I couldn't get to sleep for ages. It was too damn quiet. And every noise I did hear convinced me that someone was trying to get inside the house. But in the end, around three, I dropped off, only to wake up again before seven.

Exhausted, I clambered out of bed, made a rough toilet, dressed in yesterday's wrinkled and grubby clothes and went downstairs.

Rajah had beaten me to it. He was sitting at the tiny table in the kitchen sucking up a cup of tea. 'There's fresh in the pot,' he said.

I poured out a cup, added powdered milk and sugar and sat opposite him, our knees almost touching. 'We've got to get some fresh milk,' I complained. 'This powdered stuff tastes like shit.'

'We'll have to get some food too,' he replied. 'We'll take a ride later.'

'And toothpaste and soap. And a razor,' I added. 'And I need something other than this lot to wear. I've got nothing thanks to you.'

'You couldn't go home,' he said. 'You don't know who might have been waiting.'

That was true at least. 'At least I could've got some cash,' I said.

He grinned. 'I told you I've got enough.' He pulled a a fat wallet out of his jacket pocket and riffled through a wad of fifty-pound notes that stuck out of the top. 'Just relax.'

'Any sign of the children?' I asked.

'No. Not yet. Let them sleep.'

'And then what?' I asked. 'Seriously. There seems to be no solution to this mess apart from them getting as far away from her father as possible. I mean abroad whatever she says about having the child here. Spain or somewhere. There's enough cash in that wallet for two first class flights and a bit left over till they get settled. Paul's done bar work. Even at this time of year he'd be bound to get something.'

'Or a reconciliation,' said Rajah thoughtfully.

'Fat chance by all accounts. And it won't help that both you and I have changed sides. Why, by the way?'

'Why what?'

'Why did you do it? Khan said you were one of his most trusted men.'

'I'm no one's man. And why you as well?'

'It's Meena, I suppose. I just can't help it. There's something about her you want to help. And there's my daughter. Since her mother died I've been pretty useless. She seems to be able to take care of herself without my help. Maybe it's just my way of paying something back.'

'Precisely. I had a daughter too once. Still have of course, although I doubt she'd even recognise me. She's back in India with her mother. I send money but it's not enough. We all have our demons.'

'Man, we're on a hiding to nothing here,' I said.

'We'll survive.'

'I wish I could be as certain.'

'Trust me, Mr Sharman.'

I didn't point out that that was exactly what Khan had done. Instead I said, 'Call me Nick, for Christ's sake.'

'Christ was just a prophet who got taken too seriously,' he said with a sly smile.

'And please. Don't get all philosophical on me, for Christ's... for God's sake,' I corrected myself, and smiled too.

I thought I'd try Melanie on the mobile again but all I could get was a screaming feedback through the earpiece. 'What's the matter with the bloody phone?' I said.

Rajah shrugged. 'Use the one in the car,' he said and tossed me the keys. 'But not a word about where we are.'

'I don't know where we bloody well are,' I replied. 'And I have done this before, you know.'

'Sorry,' he said.

I went outside to the Mercedes, but got the same result. I stood outside the car and sussed it out. We were surrounded on all sides by hills and a row of electricity pylons marched across the field beside us. Shit, I thought. That's all we bloody need. A blind spot.

I went back and told Rajah. 'Make your call when you go shopping.'

'Just me. I thought it was we a minute ago.'

'It's safer that way. The pair of us are too conspicuous together.'

'Safer for who? Don't forget we've got dodgy plates on that motor.'

'I'm sure you can cope.'

'Looks like I'll have to. Just make sure Paul and Meena don't make any calls on the land line. They're too easily traced these days.'

He nodded. 'Trust me,' he said again.

Fifty-seven

B Y THE TIME I left to go on my shopping trip there was still no sign of our young charges. Rajah gave me four fifty-pound notes. 'I hope these are kosher,' I said on the way out.

'You *have* got a suspicious mind.'

'I've had to in the past.'

'Don't worry, they're as good as gold.'

'I'll take your word for it.'

'Trust me.'

'There seems to be an awful lot of trust involved on my part in this.'

'It's good for the soul.'

I didn't bother to make any reply to that and went out into the chilly morning air, slid in behind the wheel of the Mercedes and tried the phone again. I punched in Melanie's number but still got no joy. I started the car up, reversed out of the drive, drove up the lane and mentally tossed a coin as to which direction to take. I chose left and passed through the village which didn't look any more awake in the cold light of day than it had the previous night, and after ten minutes found a main road, turned in the opposite direction to the way posted to Manchester, and within fifteen minutes discovered a big Sainsbury's hypermarket. I was almost disappointed. The car was so responsive and pleasant to drive I could've kept going all day. In fact I almost did.

I drove into a car park that would comfortably have taken a year's production of the Ford Motor Company and parked the Mercedes in one corner.

I went into the coolness of the building and found everything I needed from fresh socks to a bottle of Remy Martin and started loading up a trolley.

Three quarters of an hour later with Rajah's two hundred quid almost gone I went back to the car and tried Melanie again.

She was in her office. 'Where the hell are you?' she demanded. 'I've been leaving messages.'

'Well it ain't Kansas, Toto.'

'So where is it?'

'A long way from home, love, ' I replied. 'There's been a few developments.'

'Like what?'

I gave her the seven-inch version without naming places.

'Christ,' she said when I was finished.

'Big surprises all round,' I said.

'You can say that again. That bloody Rajah. He could've killed the pair of us in Manchester.'

'Not according to him,' I said. 'And he's not such a bad bloke when you get to know him.'

'I'm glad you've made a new friend.'

'They're few and far between in this world.'

'Meaning?'

'Nothing. Look I don't know how long this is going to take, and you can't reach me where I am because the bloody phones won't work.' I declined to tell her about the land line. You just never know, and the less she knew the better for all of us.

'That's convenient.'

'Hardly. We've got to drive out of the area before we can talk to anyone.'

'Like I said, that's convenient.'

'Don't be like that, Mel.'

'Oh what's the use. Call me when you can be bothered.' And she hung up with an electronic clatter.

I sighed and put the car phone back in its holster.

I drove back to the cottage, only getting lost a couple of times and reversed the Merc into the drive and up to the door. I didn't want people looking at my new undies.

Paul and Meena were up and about when I got inside, and as I brought in the bags from the supermarket they started eating. It was like an infestation of locusts.

'I can see I'm going to be a good customer,' I said to Rajah as the pair of them opened bottles and cans and packets. 'It's just as well you're holding.'

'Let them have their fun,' he said. 'They'll have to get serious soon enough.'

I knew he was right, but the knowledge gave me little pleasure.

Fifty-eight

'I'D BETTER GO and make some calls myself,' said Rajah after we'd had some more tea. This time, thank Christ, with proper whole milk in mine. Not very healthy for a man my age, I'll agree. But then nor is a bacon and egg sandwich with butter on white sliced bread. And that was exactly what I was going to make for my mid-morning snack.

'Who you gonna call?' I asked, suddenly suspicious.

'Ghostbusters!' chorused Paul and Meena.

'Very funny,' I said. 'You two don't seem to be taking this very seriously.'

'If you'd been on your own for so long, with no money and hardly enough to eat most of the time, always running scared, and now, with two big tough guys looking after you, perhaps you'd have a laugh too,' said Meena.

'Fair enough,' I said. 'Sorry. I wasn't thinking. And thanks for the compliment. But who?' I asked Rajah again.

'Just a few contacts.'

'You wouldn't be calling Khan to come and collect these two, would you?' I said. 'A nice bit of scratch in your bin, you know the deal.'

'Listen Sharman,' said Rajah. 'If I was going to sell them out I'd've done it a long time ago. And I wouldn't have intervened last night when you were about to get your pretty face kicked in. Think about it.'

I thought about it. But just for a second. 'You're right,' I said. 'Sorry.' It was definitely my morning for apologies.

'How far do you have to go to get a decent connection?' he asked as he stood up.

'Dunno. I made my call from the supermarket. It's about five miles away. It was crystal clear there. But if you drove to the top of one of those hills...'

'I'll try it,' he said and left.

I rescued the *Telegraph* from one of the shopping bags I'd brought in, left Paul and Meena to put the rest of the supplies away, either in the fridge and cupboard or in their stomachs, and went into the living room where I kicked some life into last night's fire and started on the crossword.

Rajah returned before I'd quarter finished it. 'All right?' I said when he stuck his head round the door.

'Everything's quiet.'

'Who'd you talk to?'

'Still not sure, are you?' he asked.

'Yes I'm sure,' I replied. 'I'm just curious.'

He came into the room and settled a giant ham on the arm of a chair. I was worried it would tip him into the fireplace. 'Just a couple of friends,' he said. 'People I can trust.'

I was thinking this whole thing relied too much on trust but I said nothing. 'And?' I said instead.

'Like I said, all quiet.'

'So we just sit here till the cash runs out.'

'No.' He was adamant. 'No. You're right. I think we're going to have to talk them into leaving the country. Maybe I'll go with them. Drive down to Spain. I could do with some sun.'

'Top up your tan,' I said, but I smiled as I said it. I didn't want him to get the wrong idea.

'I dunno,' he replied. 'I could get a job as a bouncer. I've done it before.'

'That doesn't surprise me,' I said. 'Except I thought they called them door security executives these days.'

'Not in the sort of place I worked,' he replied.

I was getting to like Rajah.

Meena came in from the kitchen then munching on a chocolate biscuit. 'You'll get fat,' I said.

'I *am* eating for two,' she said back.

'More like twenty-two the way you're putting the calories away,' said Rajah.

She stuck out her tongue, and that was when it occurred to me that we were getting to be like a little family, and I didn't mind it one bit. But the trouble with families is that you can get too attached to them.

And you tend to miss them once they're gone.

Fifty-nine

AND THAT'S HOW we spent the rest of the day. Eating, reading the papers and magazines I'd brought back from the supermarket and trying to watch a TV that suffered from the same problems as the mobile phones. And worse, had no remote control. Meena and I cooked dinner together. No surprise that I'd bought the makings of Indian food, and as I chopped, she sautéed and together it smelt pretty good.

Rajah came in when the food was almost ready. 'We need to talk,' he said to Meena.

'About?'

'About you and Paul and the baby. And me and Mr Sharman.'

'What about us?'

'Simple. We can't stay here. We can't even stay in the country.'

Meena's mouth set in a firm line.

'Now listen,' he said. 'I've had an idea. You want the baby to have British citizenship. So we go to Spain and when it's due we hop over to Gibraltar. Easy.'

I wondered why I'd never thought of that.

'Gibraltar,' she echoed. 'What's Gibraltar got to do with it?'

'If the baby's born there it'll be British.'

Meena looked at me, but it was no good asking. I hadn't a clue, although it sounded right. 'Of course,' I said, with a confidence I didn't really feel, and hoped it was.

'I'll drive you both down there,' said Rajah. 'Stay with you. Look after you both.'

'What about passports?' I said.

'I've got one,' replied Meena. 'Dad got me one. He was going to send me back to India. Get me away from the evil influences of the West.'

'More like the evil influences of Paul,' I said.

Meena smiled. 'Probably.'

'Have you got it with you?' I asked.

She nodded. 'But it's in my unmarried name.'

'No big deal,' said Rajah. 'They don't bother much on the way out.'

'Has Paul?' I interjected.

'Yes.'

'How about you, Rajah?' I said.

'Never go anywhere without it.'

Well that was something at least.

'See,' said Rajah. 'Simple.'

'And you can drop me off in London on the way,' I said. 'Or at any railway station.'

'I'll have to talk to Paul,' said Meena, stirring her curry sauce.

'I already did,' said Rajah. 'He's all for it.'

'Let me think about it,' said Meena.

'Of course. But don't take too long. The sooner we get out of here the better.'

I whispered a silent 'Amen' to that.

Sixty

WE ALL SAT down and discussed the matter after dinner. Me with my bottle of Remy, Rajah, Meena and Paul with bottled water and milk shakes out of little plastic bottles respectively. To each his own.

'It's the only way,' said Rajah, after we'd chased the subject around the table for half an hour.

'It's got to be,' I added. 'This way you'll be safe.'

'What are we going to do for money?' said Meena. 'And food. I've never been abroad.'

'They do eat in Spain,' said Paul. 'They're right, Meena. It'll be fun. And warm.'

'And I've got enough money for our immediate needs,' said Rajah. 'Then Paul and I'll get jobs. There's stacks of work out there.'

'I'm scared,' said Meena, touching her tummy.

'You've been scared before,' I said. 'All the time you were on the run with Paul. And you made it. You were brave. I admire the way you handled it. This way you'll be free. Rajah will take care of you.'

Rajah nodded agreement.

'I'm not sure,' she said.

'Come on, Meena,' said Paul. 'I'm sick of running. Down there we can relax. It'll be great, just you wait and see.'

She looked at each of us in turn. 'OK,' she said after a moment.

'Terrific,' I said.

'What about you?' asked Meena, looking at me with her beautiful eyes.

'I'll get by,' I said.

'What if my father comes after you?'

'He doesn't know I'm with you,' I said. 'He just thinks I quit on him. He'll get over it.'

'You could always come with us,' she said.

It had never occurred to me.

'Please. You could get work down there too,' she went on.

'I used to help out in a bar,' I said, suddenly getting into the swing of things.

'There you go,' said Paul. 'What a team we'd make.'

'I don't have my passport with me.'

'Pick it up on the way through,' said Meena.

I was tempted. 'But there's my girlfriend,' I said.

'Bring her along too,' said Rajah.

'I don't think so,' I said.

'Then get another one. There's plenty of available women in Spain.'

'That might not be a bad idea,' I said. 'The way things have been going.'

'So?' said Meena.

'All right,' I said. 'I've always fancied a warm climate.'

'Wonderful,' she said, and ran round the table kissing each of us on the cheeks in turn.

We drank a toast with our various beverages. 'Don't forget you've got those dodgy plates on your car,' I said to Rajah. 'We don't want to get nicked trying to get on the ferry.'

'They'll be fine. I can pick up a set of the right ones in any motor accessory shop. They'll make them up while we wait. I've got all the papers for the car with me.'

'You travel prepared,' I said.

'I try.'

'When are we going to go?' asked Meena.

'First thing in the morning,' replied Rajah. 'I've got to make a call. Just to make sure everything's OK. Anyway, it's too late to go tonight. Let's get some rest and start out fresh.'

We drank another toast and watched the TV picture fragment through an old movie before we all turned in to bed.

Sixty-one

WE WERE UP early the next morning, and after our last breakfast in the cottage we packed our few meagre possessions, and waited whilst Rajah went out to make his calls.

It was cool and blustery outside and black clouds chased each other across the big blue sky, and intermittently a choppy, cold rain fell. There'd been a storm in the night and lightning had lit up the sky and thunder had seemed to rock the small cottage to its very foundations. It had been like being aboard a ship at sea. I'd got up and made a cup of tea and sat drinking it in the darkness of my room, lit only by the flashes of sheet lightning as bright as a million stars, as the rain lashed down and drummed on the roof and the walls and the windows as if it was searching for me personally.

I stood in the porch and smoked a cigarette whilst I waited for Rajah to return. I didn't want to blow smoke all over Meena, her being pregnant and all.

And then, during one squall as the sun burst through the clouds and lit up the tops of hills around me, a perfect rainbow appeared, seeming to start on the tip of the closest pylon and end on the furthest one.

I couldn't believe how perfect the colours were as the bow arched clear from one side of the valley to the other.

Despite everything I smiled as I watched the rainbow, as the wind tugged at my jacket and cold drops of rain hissed on the coal of my cigarette, and I thought about what our future would be like together in the land of sun, sea and sangria.

The rainbow was beautiful and I wanted to fetch Meena and Paul to see it, but I was afraid that if I turned my back, like so many other things in my life it would vanish, leaving only dark clouds hanging over my head.

Before I could decide, I heard the hum of a powerful engine in the lane and Rajah swung the Mercedes into the drive. It slid to a halt in a shower of pebbles.

And I just knew that everything was fucked.

He jumped out of the car and I went to meet him and together we stood in the rain facing each other. His face was like the thunder that had rocked the house earlier that morning. 'It's gone wrong,' he said.

'How?'

'The cops were round my house yesterday. They were looking for suspects in a serious assault that happened in Streatham night before last.'

'So someone got the car number.'

'Obviously.'

'No big deal. We'll be in Spain by tomorrow.'

'That's not the worst. Khan's found out about Caroline Lees being in touch with Meena.'

'How?'

'Her father got it out of her. She let it slip that she knew Meena was married.'

'Shit! Stupid girl.'

'You can't really blame her. It was a big secret to keep.'

'Yeah. Then we'd better go.'

'Come on then, let's get the others.'

We walked back into the house and I shook rain from my hair. As we walked into the living room Meena was just putting down the telephone receiver.

'Meena,' I said, not believing my eyes. 'What the hell are you doing?'

She jumped and the skin on her face darkened in a blush.

'Nothing.'

'Don't tell lies,' I said. 'Who the hell were you calling?'

She hesitated. 'Come on,' I said. 'Tell us.'

'It was Caroline,' she said in a small voice. 'She wasn't there.'

'Caroline Lees,' I exploded. 'Christ, girl, your father knows she's been talking to you.'

'I'm sorry,' she said with a sob in her voice. 'I had to say goodbye. I didn't know if I'd ever see her again.'

A gust of wind moaned in the roof then, and rain beat against the window and when I looked out across the valley I saw that the rainbow was gone, and probably all our chances of a new life together.

Sixty-two

'YOU CALLED HER on that phone,' I said disbelievingly. 'An open line. Didn't Rajah tell you not to?'

She nodded.

'Then why didn't you ask to use the mobile in the car?'

'You wouldn't have let me.' She was right about that at least.

I sighed in exasperation. 'Well please tell me you masked the calls.'

She shook her head and looked at Paul who looked equally guilty, as if to ask him what I meant.

'You dial 141 before the number you want,' I explained patiently.

She just shook her head again and said, 'I didn't know.'

Jesus, I knew that she'd led a sheltered life, but this was ridiculous.

I looked at Paul then. 'But you knew about 141 didn't you?' I said.

'I didn't think,' he replied.

'How could you, Paul?' I said in exasperation. 'After all we've been through.'

'But we're leaving,' he stammered. 'I thought it would be OK. And anyway it probably wouldn't work on a museum piece like that.'

'At least tell me that this is the first time you've called her?' I said hopefully.

Meena shook her head and looked down at the floor so that her long, lustrous hair covered her face.

I wanted to tug her head up and scream into her face how stupid she'd been, but I stopped myself short. I wanted to hurt her for her thoughtlessness but I knew it was only ignorance on her part, not malice, and what good would it do? How could I hurt her anyway? The whole point of me being there was to prevent her from getting hurt.

'How many times?' I asked in a more gentle tone.

'Twice. This was the second time.'

'When did you call her first?'

'Yesterday night,' she replied after a moment.

'What time?'

'Late. After you'd all gone to bed. Midnight.'

Whilst I'd been drinking tea in my room.

I looked at my watch. It was just after eight. 'Oh Meena,' I said. 'That means they've had the number for nearly eight hours and they'll get the address from their mates in the police and they could be here any minute. They're only up the road.'

Or they could be here right now, I thought, but didn't vocalise it. By the look on Rajah's face he was thinking the same thing.

I went to the window and looked down the drive. All was quiet in the cold autumn rain, but I knew it was just a matter of time and I could taste ashes in my mouth.

'We'd better get out of here,' I said. 'We can't trust anybody but ourselves now. And we won't be safe until we're on that ferry.' The more I thought about it the better I felt about getting clear away.

'I'm sorry,' said Meena.

She was crying properly now and Paul knelt by her side. 'Don't worry, sweetheart,' he said.

'Come on,' I said and went to Meena's side and offered her my hand. 'Up you get. It's done now and maybe this exchange isn't digitalised and they can't trace the call. The main thing is that we've got to get out of here sharpish. This place is blown. Get your stuff and let's go.'

Paul ran upstairs to get his and Meena's things and I went up after him to my room for my spare pack of cigarettes and my dirty clothes which I'd stuffed into a Sainsbury's bag. When I came back down, Rajah was standing in the tiny hallway all but filling it to capacity. 'Don't bother,' he said. 'Someone's done the motor.'

Sixty-three

'WHAT?' I SAID disbelievingly.
'The tyres, the ignition, and they've nicked the phone.'
'Thorough,' I said.
'They always are.'
'What about the guns?'
He shook his head. 'Gone.'
'Shit,' I said. 'I told you we should've brought them inside.'
He just shrugged in that way of his.
'Didn't you hear them?'
'Not a thing. They're good.'
'As good as us?'
'They found us, didn't they?'
'No fault of ours.'
'Maybe, maybe not.'
'Shit. Do Meena and Paul know?'
He shook his mighty head in reply.
But they soon will, I thought as I heard Paul walk along the corridor above us.
'Just as well I've got this then, isn't it?' I said, and produced the Browning 9mm I'd removed from the Mercedes boot whilst out on my trip to the supermarket and that I'd kept tucked down the back of my jeans ever since. Plus I'd loaded two spare clips from the box of ammunition. Amazing what you can get at Sainsbury's these days. If that wasn't enough ammunition to get me through the day, then I wasn't the shootist I thought I was.
'What … ?' exclaimed Rajah.
'I just feel safer with something like this under my pillow at night,' I said. 'Makes me feel all warm and secure.'
'Gimme,' he said, waggling his podgy fingers at me.
'Fuck off, pal,' I said. 'Finders keepers, losers weepers.'
'I could take it.'
'You could've had the lot if you'd listened to me.'
'You're a sly bastard, Sharman,' he said.
'But I think ahead.'

With that the three of us rejoined Meena in the living room. 'Bad news, sweetheart,' I said. 'They're here.'

Meena cried out in fear and Paul pulled her close.

'What are we going to do?' asked Meena, her voice shaking with panic.

I told her of my plan to call the police.

'You can't,' she cried. 'You know what happened when we went to the police before.'

'They're here, Meena,' I said as calmly as I possibly could. 'We don't know what the hell they're going to do. At least the police won't hurt you.'

'But they'll deliver us back to the family,' said Paul. 'And you know what her father's threatened to do.'

I didn't reply.

'We're going to have to do something,' said Rajah. 'Eventually they're going to come in here after us.'

'Then it's the police or nothing,' I said and went into the living room and picked up the phone. It was dead. I jiggled the buttons on top to no avail. 'So it's nothing,' I said and tossed the dead instrument into the fireplace in frustration.

Sixty-four

'So what do we do?' asked Paul, when he'd joined us and we'd told him what was going on.

'There's only one thing for it,' I said. 'One of us will have to go out the back, across the garden and into the field at the end. Straight across is the lane to the main road and there's a phone box on the corner. It's pretty well hidden by trees and with any luck they won't have noticed it and smashed it up.'

'You hope,' said Paul.

'Hope is about all we've got left,' I said. 'We've gone about as far as we can running away.'

'*I* hope we've got that much time before they come for us,' said Rajah.

'Well we've just got to hope that luck's with us and the cops get here first,' I said. I was getting pretty pissed off by their negativity.

'Who's going to go?' asked Paul.

'Me, I suppose,' I said. 'It looks like it's my gig.'

'How long?' he asked.

I went to the window and peered through again. All was quiet and the clouds were gathering again. Dark clouds that heralded another storm. 'Soon,' I said. 'I think it's going to rain hard again soon. That'll be the best time.'

'That might be too late.'

'No,' I said. 'Let's wait for the storm. They won't be able to see if the rain's as heavy as it was last night. If I get caught, then we're buggered.'

'And what happens when the police do arrive?' asked Meena.

'We throw ourselves on their mercy,' I said. 'Not every copper in the land is hand in glove with your family. We go with them and regroup. We haven't done anything wrong. Apart from that punch-up in London and nicking a set of number plates. Hardly hanging offences either of them. And with any luck, when they show, whoever's out there will just vanish. We need transport and communication. And for that we need some kind of civilisation.'

'And if the cops just tell us to piss off?' said Paul.

'Then we give them some other reason to arrest us. Nothing serious, just so's we get away from here.'

'Risky,' said Rajah.

'You got any better ideas?' I demanded. 'We're in enough trouble as it is, I'd rather face a night in the cells and a bit of police bail than a run in with Meena's brothers.'

I looked at their faces and none of the trio came up with an argument. 'So it's agreed then,' I said.

One by one they nodded.

Sixty-five

'MEANWHILE WE'D BETTER keep alert,' I said. 'Rajah. You want to go upstairs, see what you can see? Maybe we'll get an idea how many of them there are.'

Rajah nodded and left the room and I heard his heavy footsteps on the stairs. 'I'll take the kitchen and check the back,' said Paul. 'Meena. You stay here with Nick. OK, Nick?'

'Fine by me,' I said and lit a cigarette. The condemned man and all that. 'I hope you don't mind,' I said to Meena.

'No,' she replied. 'If I wasn't in the family way I'd have one myself.' She sat on the sofa and hummed to herself as I perched on the window ledge and watched the gloom from the dark sky thicken across the front garden through the net curtains.

All was quiet. And a bloody good job as far as I was concerned.

The rain came about ten minutes later and it was almost as dark as evening outside. I slid off my uncomfortable perch and went to the door. 'Rajah,' I shouted. 'Paul. It's time I got going.'

I heard movement from upstairs and went into the kitchen, which was empty. 'Paul,' I called again, but no answer came and I knew, even before I tried the back door that opened at a touch, that he was gone. I ran back into the hall and Rajah was on the stairs. 'Did you see anything?' I asked.

'No.'

'Were you watching the back?'

'Back and front.'

But of course he couldn't have watched both at once.

'Shit,' I said.

'What?'

'In here, quick,' I said. I didn't want Meena to hear.

He followed me into the kitchen.

'Paul's gone,' I said.

'Gone where?'

'Fuck knows. But I'd give it a good guess. The silly sod's gone to the phone, I bet.'

We stood together in that tiny, cold room and considered the wreckage of our brave attempt to help the couple.

'Damn,' said Rajah, and as he turned to leave I saw a tiny red dot appear on the collar of his jacket and slowly move up to his neck.

'Rajah!' I screamed and leapt at him, knocking him into one of the cupboards which his great bulk reduced to matchwood.

'What the—' he screamed back as we fell together, but his voice was almost drowned by the crash of the kitchen window imploding, showering us with glass, and the twin thumps as the bullets smacked into the wall beside us almost shaking the house to its foundations. Whoever had liberated the silenced Uzi kept firing and the bullets smashed through the kitchen door as if it had been made of papier mâché and carried on through the connecting wall to the room where Meena was waiting.

'Meena,' I yelled. 'Get down! Down on the floor now,' as I clawed the Browning from the back of my belt and bobbed up, firing three bullets into the garden in what I hoped was the general direction that we'd been fired upon.

Then, when I heard a scream from Meena in the front room I thought at first that she'd been hit. But when she screamed again, a scream that called Paul's name, I knew that I'd been right all along, and that everything had gone wrong.

Sixty-six

Rajah and I ran into the living room and saw Meena at the window, one hand at her mouth. Looking out over her shoulder I saw her brothers and two other Asians I'd not seen before standing at the end of the drive. The strangers were big blokes. Not as big as Rajah but big enough. One wore a long black macintosh, the other a leather bomber jacket. They were all armed. Macintosh was toting the AK47, Bomber Jacket had the Desert Eagle. Sanjay was holding a vicious looking knife to Paul's throat in his left hand. His right arm was around Meena's husband's chest, and in that hand was one of the guns I'd been shown in the restaurant back in Manchester. Deepak had *his* niner hanging down by his side. Daddy wasn't around to hold them in check and I imagined this time they were prepared to use the guns. The fact that Bomber Jacket had shot at Rajah through the kitchen window rather confirmed that. I dropped the magazine out of the Browning and inserted a fresh clip with fourteen bullets in it and worked the action. 'Shit,' I said. 'I hope he made it to the phone box before they got him.'

'Is that all you can think of,' hissed Meena. 'Can't you see that it's his bravery in going for help that has got him into the hands of my brothers and their gang. If you'd gone when he said, it would be you out there.'

'Cheers,' I said. 'But maybe if he'd waited like I said, none of us would've been captured. Now he's just a hostage to all our fortunes.'

'All supposing he *was* going to the phone box,' said Rajah.

'And not running away.'

'He wouldn't,' said Meena.

'I tend to agree there,' I said. 'I don't think he'd leave Meena and the baby. Not after what they've gone through so far. But that's not the issue. The issue *is* what do we do now?'

Meena answered that for me. Before Rajah and I could stop her, she'd darted through to the hall and out of the front door. 'Leave him be,' she shouted to Sanjay once she was on the path.

'For Christ's sake,' I said. 'What *is* she like?'

Rajah didn't make any philosophical comment this time: he just went out after her leaving me and my Browning alone in the house.

I looked through the window at the tableau outside and decided I'd better get in on the act.

Sixty-seven

'STOP WHERE YOU are,' I heard Sanjay call to Meena and Rajah as I reached the open front door, and saw him pull the knife tighter against Paul's Adam's apple. It was a flat-bladed weapon that caught the sun as it came out from behind a cloud. It had stopped raining by then, but water dripped from the trees and sparkled on the paintwork of Rajah's Mercedes as it sat on its four flat tyres in front of us. 'Rajah, you traitor, you're a dead man. Throw down your gun,' said Sanjay.

From my vantage point I saw the big man open his hands to show they were empty.

'You fired out the back, I know you're armed. Now give it up or I'll shoot.' This time Deepak spoke.

Definitely time for me to make an appearance. I stepped through the door, the Browning pointing skywards and said, 'He's telling the truth.'

'Sharman,' said Deepak. 'What the hell are you doing here?'

'Just came along for the ride.'

'That's something you're going to regret. Throw down the gun.'

'No,' I replied bringing the Browning down to point in their direction. 'You lot throw down your guns.' I supposed there'd be no shooting from their side when Meena was in the firing line and I just hoped that my supposition was correct.

Deepak looked at Sanjay and laughed. 'You're joking.'

'I've never been more serious in my life,' I said.

'We'll kill you.'

'Will you? Killed a lot of people, have you?' Our only chance was wrongfooting them and trusting that the cops had been called and weren't far away.

The look on Sanjay's face told me he hadn't.

'I thought not,' I said. 'There's a lot more to shooting at live targets than posing around in front of a mirror with your dick in your hand.'

'That remains to be seen.'

'Take my word for it.'

I moved closer to where Meena was standing. 'Keep still,' said Deepak.

I shook my head and he raised his gun.

'Listen,' I said. 'Let Meena go. She could get hurt.'

'If providence means it to be.'

Jesus, another fucking philosopher. What was with these geezers?

'Kill him,' he said to Sanjay.

At first, whether he meant me, Paul or Rajah wasn't clear. But whoever, it was too much for Meena. 'No!' she screamed and made to run towards the group, but I caught her arm and pulled her to me. 'Let me go,' she cried.

'Stay here,' I said. 'And be quiet.'

'She never listens,' said Deepak. 'Surely you must know that by now.'

'Sanjay,' I said calmly. 'Let Meena go. Let Paul go. There's no need for this. They're not up to this.'

'No,' he replied. 'Our sister maybe. But not him. He betrayed our friendship like the snake he is. He violated our sister. He deserves to die.'

'No he doesn't,' I said.

'Please Sanjay,' Meena wept. 'Please.'

Paul shouted. 'I made the call.'

'Then it's all over, Sanjay,' I said. 'The police are on their way. Can't we just talk about it?'

'There's been enough talk. We're out in the wilds,' he replied. 'They've got a long way to come.'

'But they'll get here eventually. Why don't you just admit that Paul and Meena are together. They're married now.'

'Not in our religion they're not,' he sneered. 'And they never will be.'

'Let him go,' Meena shouted as she struggled in my grasp. 'He's my husband. I love him.'

'What do you know of love?' said Deepak.

'I'm having his baby,' she said. 'I know that much.'

'His baby, you whore,' said Sanjay, his face visibly paling to a nasty shade of grey. 'How could you do such a thing? I'll kill him first then cut the bastard out of your belly.' And with a flick of his wrist he cut Paul's throat and a huge gout of blood poured down his chest.

It happened so suddenly as the sun vanished behind a cloud again, that for a second I didn't believe I'd seen it.

'Noooo,' Meena howled like an animal in pain and went limp in my grasp.

Sanjay dropped Paul to the drive and stood back proudly, a stain of gore shining on his sleeve.

'Bastard,' said Rajah and started towards him.

All four guns came up and I knew that it was within a hair of going off. Meena was slumped back against me in a faint and I couldn't get into a firefight with her acting like a human shield, so I grabbed her round the waist and threw her to the ground, rolling under the lowered body of the Merc, dragging her with me through the mud and feeling the rough edges of the undercarriage cut into my shoulders.

Macintosh fired the AK47 in our direction, chopping up the surface of the driveway then slamming into the bodywork of the car as I wrestled my gun round.

Then the others started firing together, so that it was only ballistics that could later work out who shot whom. Macintosh kept the machine-gun pointed in my and Meena's direction until the thirty-shot clip ran out. That took just one pull on the trigger. Bomber Jacket tried for us too, but thankfully the Mercedes had been made of high grade steel and kept most of the bullets within itself: the interior got sliced to ribbons as I saw later when I examined the remains of the car. Sanjay and Deepak fired at Rajah, both compulsively pulling the trigger time after time. The pathologist found seventeen entrance holes in his body. Such was the range and the power of the brothers' guns that all but three shots passed through his body, massive though he was. Out of the corner of my eye I saw the slugs chop the great man down to the ground sending ribbons of blood flying out from his back as the bullets chewed their way through him.

I fired the Browning once, hit Deepak in the side, changed aim slightly and hit Sanjay somewhere in his chest. The Browning felt good in my hand. Warm and comfortable like an old friend. Meanwhile Macintosh had thrown the Kalashnikov to the ground and was reaching for something under his coat when I let him have a couple of bullets in the midsection that knocked him to the ground, so that left only Bomber Jacket, who was keeping up fire from the apparently endless supply of .44 shells in his Uzi. Bullets were smacking into the ground all around us as I double-tapped again and saw his head explode like a watermelon as both bullets hit him in the face.

All this had taken less than ten seconds.

I slid out from under the car, pulling Meena behind me. She opened her eyes and I wished she hadn't. It was the perfect time for her to remain unconscious. I stood up and looked at the six bodies scattered around the drive. Three of them seemed to be still breathing. Three were definitely beyond saving. Unfortunately it was obvious Paul and Rajah were two of the latter. Meena joined me. 'Is Paul all right?' she asked in a small voice. I checked his vital signs but I knew it was hopeless just by the amount of blood he'd shed. I stood up again and shook my head at Meena, and somewhere far off I heard the whoop of police sirens.

And then to make a perfect day complete Rajesh Khan walked into view. 'My God,' he gasped. 'What happened?'

'Are you satisfied now?' I demanded. 'The man that Meena loved and one of your best friends are dead. And this man too.' I pointed down at Bomber Jacket. 'And your sons and the other one may be soon if we don't get help. Is that enough for you?'

'I didn't mean for this to happen.'

'What *did* you expect? You told me they were beyond your control at the start of all this.'

'That's why I sent Mohammed and Benjamin to help them.'

'Whilst you stayed nice and safe and warm in the car. Whichever of you survive will be in the dock if I have any say in the matter. This doesn't end here.' I indicated him, his sons and the other two gangsters with a sweep of my arm. 'You're all guilty.'

'We have good lawyers,' he said. 'The best that money can buy.'

'MONEY!' I heard Meena screech from behind me and I saw her rise, the knife that had killed Paul in her hand. She must have picked it up from where her brother dropped it, and with more speed than I gave her credit for she ran towards her father and plunged the blade into his chest over and over again until I managed to pull her off, blood staining her clothes.

The sirens were getting louder by then so I wiped the Browning down with the tail of my shirt and pressed it into Rajah's hand putting his finger on the trigger. 'Thanks, my friend,' I whispered. 'You know I'd do the same for you.'

I stood, threw the spare clips into the undergrowth and I was just tucking my shirt in again when the first police cars entered the road outside.

I did nothing to prevent Meena's attack or help to save Khan.

It seemed like justice of a kind that his daughter killed him.

Sixty-eight

S ANJAY, DEEPAK AND the other gangster survived to go to court. Sanjay was charged with the murder of Paul Jeffries and Rajah. Deepak was a co-defender. The other gangster was charged with being an accessory. There was some confusion about who had shot the pair of them and killed the other one. The three Asians claimed it was me and I denied it, citing the fact that Rajah had been found with a smoking pistol in his hand and I was unarmed. The cops tried some tests on me to find out if I'd recently fired a gun, but they were inconclusive. I stuck with the story that I'd hidden under Rajah's Mercedes protecting Meena and her unborn child. The car was full of enough bullets to confirm that. I had a good brief and between us we brazened it out. Meena was in no condition to confirm or deny my story and eventually it all went away.

I put on a suit and tie to appear for the prosecution at the Old Bailey. The verdict was guilty. Sanjay and Deepak got life, the other one got twelve years. It was a decent result.

Mrs Jeffries and Peter Jeffries were there. She followed me into the big hall and thanked me for doing what I'd done for her son and his wife.

I was ashamed that I hadn't done better and I told her so.

She put her hand on my sleeve and thanked me again. 'At least you were there,' she said. 'You tried.'

I covered her hand with mine, then I looked back as I walked away and saw that she was crying. Peter Jeffries ignored me and I never saw or spoke to him again.

And as for Meena. She never got over seeing Paul and Rajah being killed in that short, desperate battle, and then killing her own father. She was found unfit to plead and sent to a secure medical facility in Cheshire to have her baby. I visited her once after the birth. I caught a minicab from the railway station in the nearest town. It was spring by then, and as we drove through the countryside there were lambs in the fields and daffodils were bending in the cold breeze coming off the Irish Sea. At one point a track from the Bay City Rollers came on the radio that the cab driver was playing softly in the front and it reminded me of Rajah. I'd grown fond of him in those few short days we'd been together in that chilly cottage, and I missed him.

I told the cabbie to wait on the turnaround outside the imposing gates of the hospital. After I'd shown the bloke in the gatehouse the visitor's order that the doctor who was treating Meena had sent me, I walked up the long drive to the building and was shown to the visitors' room where the lino was scuffed, and the rugs scattered over it were all crumby and covered with cigarette burns and dried, shiny pieces of chewing gum. Meena came in with a nurse in attendance but I don't think she recognised me, and her once bright eyes were dull and lustreless.

We sat in front of a picture window that looked over the grounds, her baby, a boy named after his father, in a carrycot beside us.

Meena never spoke, just hummed a nameless tune the whole time and after an hour of listening I left.

I haven't seen her since and don't go to Suri's restaurant any more. Melanie wouldn't see me after all the media attention and eventually found someone else who can give her the kind of life she wants.

So that was that. Meena's husband, father and protector dead. Her child in care. She herself under medical supervision. Her brothers in jail, and me all alone again.

There's nothing like a fucking happy ending.